About the Author

Rob is a British Citizen who was born in Syria in the relative calm of the post-colonial, post WWII era. He read Architecture at Aleppo University and Edinburgh Art College but then pursued a career in industry and graduated from Cranfield University with an MSc in Aircraft Design. Rob lives in Japan with his Japanese wife.

Dedication

To Kyoko

Rob Domloge

Baby Samuel

AUSTIN MACAULEY
PUBLISHERS LTD.

A CIP catalogue record for this title is available from the British Library.

ISBN 9781786296870 (Paperback)
ISBN 9781786296887 (Hardback)
ISBN 9781786296894 (E-Book)

www.austinmacauley.com

First Published (2016)
Austin Macauley Publishers Ltd.
25 Canada Square
Canary Wharf
London
E14 5LQ

[from Wikipedia]

Uncle Sam (initials U.S.) is a common national personification of the American government or the United States in general that, according to legend, came into use during the War of 1812 and was supposedly named for Samuel Wilson.

The 87th United States Congress adopted the following resolution on September 15, 1961: *"Resolved by the Senate and the House of Representatives that the Congress salutes Uncle Sam Wilson of Troy, New York, as the progenitor of America's national symbol of Uncle Sam."*

Foreword by the Author

I was born and brought up in Syria.

The Syria that I knew and loved, was a far cry from the tormented, mutilated country that is Syria today.

As a child, I used to read beautifully produced glossy magazines, in Arabic, about 'life in America'; America was to me a benign dreamland that beckoned.

As a young teenager watching the unfolding political drama in the Middle East in the 1960s, the role of the US often seemed unfair and at odds with the dreamland image.

Then, at the verge of adulthood I made my way to Europe. My first instinct was to breathe freer air and find out what lay beyond the politics of hatred, wars and lies. What I found was Power Politics, and one particularly dominant power. In the Middle East, whose politics I knew well, and where even more drama and tragedy was brewing, I found thumbprints of a meddling USA everywhere: as instigator, sponsor or arbiter, not always fairly, often unwisely, and rarely with any maturity. The picture of the dreamland of my childhood was fading fast.

Fascination with world economics came later when I first lived in Japan. It was the mid-1980s and the Japanese economic miracle was still in its stride, with Japanese investors buying up Manhattan, Industry Study

Tours to Japan from the US and Europe in vogue, and with some pundits even talking about the Japanese economy overtaking the USA's. And yet, with all that economic might, Japan was simply following in the slipstream of the US economy. I could not understand why the Nikkei index always followed the Dow Jones: it so closely followed it that you would think there was a string linking the two indices! The economic might of the US, it turns out, was a direct match to its dominant political power.

And then there were the 9/11 terrorist attacks. It was the aftermath of those attacks that focused my attention on the military might of the US, which, combined with the political power and the economic might, fashioned a hegemon like no other in history. A hegemon, what's more, which was ill-equipped to bring order to a disorderly world, whose charge it stealthily assumed. A hegemon which arguably reached its zenith at the onset of the economic and financial crisis of 2008.

Thus was born the concept of this book. This allegorical tale is about history but it is not a history book. It is about politics and power, but not a political thesis. It is about economics and globalisation, but not an economics analysis. It is written in a light style but with serious undertones. I wish it to entertain, but also to explain and throw light. It may not provide any answers, but may just help to ask the right questions.

In this book I wanted to offer a view of history, and not a little clue to the future.

RD

PROLOGUE

You are about to enter the magical world of VillageAll.

In a magical world everything is not what it seems and you can get lost. So I will whisper a few words in your ear so you can find your way around.

First I want to tell you about the houses. Because they really aren't houses at all. Think of a house as a country, and the husband as the officialdom, the establishment, the wife as the culture, the populace. See if husband and wife agree with each other: if they don't there may be trouble. If the house is big think of a powerful nation. If it has a garden think of colonies.

Then I will whisper something about food. When you hear food in VillageAll think money, and if people are sick, think trouble in the economy, the money markets crisis.

And one more thing: in VillageAll time stops …

But time never stops, right?

Now you are ready … here you go.

CHAPTER I

Once upon a time there was a village right by a very large river.

The village was called VillageAll.

It was called VillageAll because it had all there was.

Well, almost all.

VillageAll had all the people that there were.

Well, almost all the people. Because there were other people, but nobody knew where they lived, and nobody really cared about them. And VillageAll had all the houses that there were. Well, almost all the houses. Because there were other houses but they were very small and in places no one visited.

VillageAll had only one street, called The StreetAll, which ran by the river which flowed down from the hills and emerged from the woods at a clearing called StartAll. The river ran along the length of the village, curving away to form a large green field, which in time became the village common. The river left the village at the other end at a place called EndAll where a sharp rocky ridge rose high and the river turned into white water as it narrowed and rushed among rocks and then disappeared into a deep ravine.

The people of VillageAll never crossed the river. Well, it was a big river, and not easy to cross. And, well, everybody agreed they didn't want to cross the river, because they didn't know what there was on the other side and, anyway, they had everything they needed on the village side of the river.

So the houses of VillageAll were all built along one side of The StreetAll. They started at the First End, which was the best end of the village because it had the best air and water. The other end of VillageAll was the Far End. It was called Far End because it was far from First End and not many people went there.

At Number One, The StreetAll, lived Mr & Mrs Smith.[1] Number One was the biggest house. It had the biggest garden. Mr & Mrs Smith were a nice couple and well-liked by the people of VillageAll, especially the people who lived in First End.

Mr Smith was tall with a slight stoop, which made him look kind even though he often had a bad temper. Mr Smith was also clever and had more ideas than most of his neighbours. Mrs Smith was a very good wife and took good care of Mr Smith, the whole family and their big house. Mr & Mrs Smith had very nice clothes and when they did wear them they looked elegant. But Mr & Mrs Smith didn't often wear their nice clothes, so all the people of First End thought that the Smiths looked rather shabby.

Next to the Smiths lived Mr & Mrs Pompidou[2] in Number Two. Mr & Mrs Pompidou had many friends and their house was nearly as big as Number One, but the garden was quite a bit smaller. Mr & Mrs Pompidou had the best flowers in their garden, even though they often allowed too many weeds to grow, so their garden didn't always look beautiful. Mr Pompidou was as clever as Mr Smith but didn't have as many good ideas, but when Mr Pompidou had a good idea it was very, very good. Mostly Mr Pompidou had ideas about himself, his family and his house, but he told Mrs Pompidou that he didn't want to talk to anybody about his ideas because nobody would understand them. Mr & Mrs Pompidou wore only nice clothes, so everybody in First End thought they were very elegant and wanted to dress like them.

The Smith and Pompidou families knew each other from very long ago, and although they didn't mind living next to each other they often quarrelled and when they did everybody in First End was drawn into their argument. Well, almost everybody, because some of the families in First End didn't really like quarrelling and taking sides, so they just pretended not to see or hear anything.

The next group of houses were a little smaller but quite similar in appearance to Number One and Number Two. In them lived the Schmidts[3], Luigis[4], De Graffs[5], Anderssons[6], Cortezes[7], Spiros[8] and others.

The Cortez family lived in Number Three, The StreetAll. The Cortezes' house was quite small even

13

though the family included aunts, uncles, nephews and nieces, but they had made extensions into their garden, which was almost as large as the Smiths' garden. Mr Cortez was small and chubby. He had a smiling round face with twinkling eyes that made him look friendly. But Mr Cortez was often angry with his family and sometimes upset his cousins by telling them they were too small and they should be taller! Mr Cortez always told his wife that if he was as tall as Mr Smith or Mr Pompidou, the Cortezes would be living in Number One or Number Two instead of Number Three.

The Schmidts lived in Number Four. Mr Schmidt was not tall but was not small either. He was a stocky, strongly built man. Mr Schmidt had strong opinions and would not do anything except the 'right way'. Mr Schmidt's neighbours were not happy because they said that Mr Schmidt's 'right way' was not always right, and that it was not fun to always do things right. But this didn't worry Mr Schmidt and he always said that he didn't want to have fun because he only wanted to do serious things. The Schmidts had the biggest piano in the whole of VillageAll and often invited their friends and sang to them; everybody in VillageAll thought that both Mr & Mrs Schmidt sang the most beautiful songs in VillageAll. Well, almost everybody, because Mrs Pompidou, who was also a good singer and had a piano of her own, said, "If Mrs Schmidt worried less about singing and more about cooking, the Schmidts would be a lot more like us and a lot less like the Smiths, and that would be the best thing for First End."

Mr & Mrs Luigi lived in Number Five, The StreetAll. Although the Luigis' house was not big, Mrs Luigi liked to remind Mr Luigi that their house was the first one built in First End and that all the other houses were just imitations of the Luigi house, of course with the exception of the Smiths' house because the Smiths always had to do things their own way! Mrs Luigi had a big piano and she was a good player and singer, and often said that it was not fair that Mrs Schmidt had the biggest piano in VillageAll because if Mrs Luigi had a singing competition with Mrs Schmidt, she would always win!

Mr & Mrs Spiros lived near the end of First End and although their house was small and they had no garden, Mrs Spiros liked to remind Mr Spiros that their house was built even before the Luigis' house, and long before First End was First End!

In the last house in First End lived the Popov[9] family. Because it was the last house in First End, it was very close to Middle End, and sometimes neither the Popovs, nor their neighbours knew whether the Popovs lived in First End or Middle End!

The Popovs' house was quite big but they had almost no garden. Mr Popov was a big man, the tallest man in First End, heavily built with a body full of muscles. He had bright staring eyes with enormous eyebrows, rosy cheeks and a hearty laugh. Mr Popov was a good man and didn't want to have trouble with his neighbours, but when he frowned, his staring eyes and enormous eyebrows made him look very angry. And because Mr

Popov was so big, and because he lived away from most of the houses in First End, many people in First End were frightened of him and thought he was a bully. So although Mr Popov didn't want to quarrel with anybody, he often found himself in fights and quarrels with people in First and Middle End.

The Popov family was large and merry and they too liked music and often sang together.

The village common was quite large, large enough for all the people of VillageAll. But not many people from Middle End, and nobody from Far End, ever used it because it was near First End and, well, because the people of First End liked to use it so much for walks and picnics and what have you, so in time all the people thought it belonged to First End. Well, almost all, because sometimes there were other people who used the common. These people didn't belong to VillageAll. Nobody knew where they came from, and nobody wanted to know because these people were different. They were small and didn't wear many clothes. They would suddenly appear on the common at the riverside. They fished in the river and cooked the fish at the edge of the common. They didn't talk to anybody, and nobody talked to them or went near them. And then they would suddenly disappear. The people of First End called these people the Nomans[10].

Further down The StreetAll there was Middle End. It was called Middle End because it was in the middle of The StreetAll. The houses in Middle End were a little different from those in First End because this was the oldest part of the village, and the people who lived in this part were the first to live in the village. The houses were quite big but had no gardens and they had few windows.

The Osman[11] family lived in Number One Hundred. Everybody in Middle End thought that the Osman family lived in Middle End. Well, almost everybody, because the Osmans themselves thought they lived in First End. You see, their house was really half in First End, and half in Middle End, and well, they liked First End better. Mr Osman was a strong-headed fellow and liked to do things his own way, and although he liked First End he often quarrelled with Mr Popov, who was his closest neighbour in First End.

Mr & Mrs Mustapha[12] were the closest neighbours of the Osmans in Middle End, and lived in Number One Hundred and One. Mr & Mrs Mustapha were kind to their neighbours even though they had very little food and they had a lot of children, who were quite noisy at times.

Close to the Mustapha family lived the Pahalvan[13] family. The three families were all quite friendly to each other, and their quarrels, when they happened, didn't affect other people around them.

Mr & Mrs Singh[14] lived in Number One Hundred and Fifty. The Singhs were a very large family, but they were very poor and often didn't have enough food for all the family even though Mr & Mrs Singh worked hard every day.

In the middle of Middle End lived Mr & Mrs Ndiaye[15]. Their house was in the middle of Middle End but it had no number and nobody thought the Ndiayes lived in Middle End because their house was far from the other houses of Middle End. The Ndiaye family was very poor and lived in the smallest house of VillageAll. They had no garden of their own. But Mr & Mrs Ndiaye liked to grow flowers, and they wanted to have a small fruit tree so their children could sometimes eat fruit. So Mr & Mrs Ndiaye planted some flowers and a small fruit tree in front of their house. But the flowers and the tree were too close to the road, and passers-by in The StreetAll, especially from First End, but also some from Middle End, stepped on their flowers and bumped into their tree[16]. No matter how much they tended their flowers and their tree Mr & Mrs Ndiaye could never make them grow!

Towards the other end of The StreetAll there was Far End. The houses were large and surrounded by high walls with inner courts but had no gardens.

Mr & Mrs Chen[17] lived in Number Two Hundred. The Chens were a large family with many, many children. But the Chens were not poor, so they could look after their children and keep them well-fed and clothed. The Chens were also a very old family and one of the first to live in the village.

Next to the Chens lived Mr & Mrs Kim[18]. They were a small, quiet family and their house was quite a bit smaller than their neighbour's. Although the Kims' house was small it was pretty and full of light.

Close to the Chens and Kims lived Mr & Mrs Phong[19], Mr & Mrs Panya[20], Mr & Mrs Garudho[21], Mr & Mrs Aung[22] and Mr & Mrs Khemera[23].

Right at the end of The StreetAll lived Mr & Mrs Watanabe[24] at Number One Thousand. The Watanabes' house was not so big and not so small, and it had a beautiful but unusual garden. The garden was unusual because it was inside the house, so it was not easy to know which part was the house and which part was the garden!

The Watanabes were very quiet, very clean and they ate the best food in VillageAll. But the Watanabes' house was very strange because it had no front door! And that meant that nobody visited the Watanabes, and that the Watanabes visited nobody[25].

CHAPTER II

The people of VillageAll lived in peace and harmony. Well, almost in peace, and not always in harmony. Because there were sometimes things which some people wanted to do which other people didn't think right. But they always found a way to get back to their harmony.

Especially if it was a problem like when the Smiths wanted to take a bit of the village common[26] to add to their garden because Mr Smith said he enjoyed gardening so much. Well, it was a problem because the Smiths' neighbours also wanted to have bigger gardens, especially the Pompidou, Cortez and De Graff families who had smaller gardens than the Smiths.

Well, what can you do? The Smiths were such nice people and had lots of food and friends, and the village common happened to be nearest their house.

Even though their neighbours, the Pompidous, would not agree, (Mrs Pompidou saying to her husband, "Why can't the Smiths have a small garden like us?" and Mr Pompidou answering, "Well, my dear I could not agree more, although there is no denying that Mr Smith is much better at weeding!"), the rest of the people of First

End finally agreed to let the Smiths expand their already big garden to include the biggest part of the common, and let the Pompidous, Cortezes and De Graffs split the remaining part between them to add to their gardens. Of course nobody thought of what the Nomans might think or do once all of the common was shared like this!

And once there was a quarrel when the Luigi and Cortez families said that the Smiths should not paint their front door black[27]. They said that all houses in the First End had always had white front doors and black was not a nice colour. Well, Mr Smith had just opened VillageAll's first ever smith shop[28] and everybody in First End was excited about the things that Mr Smith could make for them, in black as well as white colours. Everybody agreed that Mr Smith had a good taste in colours. So, even though their neighbours, the Pompidous, were not very happy, (Mrs Pompidou saying to her husband, "Why can't the Smiths paint their front door white like us?" and Mr Pompidou answering, "Well, my dear I could not agree more, although I have to say that the Cortezes' and Luigis' colour sense is much worse than even the Smiths!") the village agreed that the Smiths could paint their front door black.

There was also the time when the Schmidts and the De Graffs *and* the Smiths were unhappy because, they said, "Mrs Pompidou sang so loudly that even the birds on the trees were startled and flew away!" Well, what can you do? Mrs Pompidou was such a charming lady and such a good singer. And even though Mr Pompidou didn't really mind if Mrs Pompidou would be a little quieter, he said he was very angry because their neighbours, especially the Smiths, could not sing any songs at all and the birds fell ill whenever any of them tried to sing! The Luigi and Cortez families said that they, and their birds, enjoyed Mrs Pompidou's singing and wanted her to sing louder. Well, Mrs Pompidou was so pleased, and decided that in future she would do her loud singing while visiting the Luigis and Cortezes, so that nobody could complain anymore.

Then there were the quarrels between Mr Osman and Mr Popov over Mr Osman's water pipe[29]. Mr Popov liked to take long walks in the back lanes between First End and Middle End, and he often had to go by the Osmans' house. Mr Osman would be smoking his water pipe in his garden by the road, and Mr Popov said that the smell was too strong for him and he would shout, and sometimes even swear, at Mr Osman. Well, you can say the two were not very friendly!

Although people in both Middle End and Far End also had quarrels, it seems that in recent times people in First End had the most frequent and largest quarrels.

But by and by the people of VillageAll learnt to live and get on together, and after each quarrel they made up and promised to be more careful the next time.

CHAPTER III

VillageAll always had plenty of food for everybody.

Well, almost always, and not the same food for everybody.

Between the VillageAll houses and the steep hills beyond, there were three large fields for growing food for the people of VillageAll. The fields were separated by deep ravines and people could not move from one field to another, and water could not be moved across fields.

The First Field belonged to First End. In it grew wheat and barley, vegetables and fruit trees. There was also a dairy farm, a pig farm and a cattle farm. Although there was plenty of food in the First Field, the food went to First End shops, only for people living in First End.

The Middle Field belonged to Middle End and in it grew wheat, rice and vegetables. There was also a sheep farm and a cattle farm. Most years there was enough food in the Middle Field, and what there was went to Middle End shops, only for people living in Middle End.

And the Far Field belonged to Far End. It grew only rice and vegetables, and there was also a chicken farm.

The food in Far Field depended on the rains more than the other fields, so some years there was enough food and other years not quite enough. The food from Far Field went to Far End shops, only for people living in Far End.

The harvest from each field was different from the other two fields, and different each year because different rain fell on each field.

So, although every year everybody in VillageAll had food, some people had plenty of food and others had little.

Although it was rare, there were years when good rain fell on all three fields, and everybody in VillageAll had plenty of food.

CHAPTER IV

One day Mrs Smith told her husband that she was going to have a baby[30]. Her husband was delighted. The Smiths already had two daughters but Mr Smith wanted to have more children because, he said, that their house is so big, and now they have such a big garden as well. Mr Smith also was secretly hoping to have a son so he could teach him about gardening and weeding and other interesting things that men do.

All the Smiths' neighbours were happy to hear the news of the pregnancy.

Well, almost all, because some neighbours said there were already too many people in VillageAll. Especially the Pompidous, who already had two sons and three daughters and complained that the Smiths only cared about their garden. Mrs Pompidou said to her husband that the Smiths do not need more children because "they are not like us." Well, Mr Pompidou agreed entirely but he also said that in his opinion it would be a good idea if the Smiths were sometimes a little more "like us".

The baby was due in the spring and the Smith family spent all winter making many preparations for the happy event. First a room was picked for the new baby and then Mr Smith made an effort to decorate the room and make it nice and cheerful.

Mrs Smith prepared a lot of new baby clothes for both indoors and outdoors. And Mr & Mrs Smith then bought a brand new pram and new furniture for the baby room. By early spring Mrs Smith's tummy was growing quite big. It was much bigger than it was when Mrs Smith was pregnant before. And by the time the baby was due Mrs Smith's tummy was huge!

But no baby arrived.

One month after the baby was due, it was still inside Mrs Smith's tummy.

The doctor said Mrs Smith was in good health, and the baby in her tummy was also in good health. So Mr Smith stopped worrying, but he had to help Mrs Smith to carry her tummy every time she moved, because she could no longer carry her tummy by herself.

By the end of spring the baby had still not arrived. Well, by then Mrs Smith's tummy was so big she could not move at all, and she had to have a stool to rest her tummy on, and everybody came to the Smiths to see her huge tummy. Well, almost everybody, because Mrs Pompidou said Mrs Smith's tummy was grotesque and she should hide it away instead of showing it off to everybody!

Mr Smith was now very worried. But the doctor said that Mrs Smith was strong and the baby in her tummy was also strong and would be born soon. So Mr Smith was less worried although he felt so tired every time he looked at the huge tummy of his wife.

Then in early summer the baby was born[31].

It was a big event in First End because everybody had been expecting the birth for a long time, even if not everybody was sure it was going to be a happy event. But it was especially a big event because when the baby was born it took its first gulp of air and then burst out in a very, very loud cry that shook the whole of First End. Everybody was saying, "Goodness … did you hear that?"

Well, almost everybody, because Mrs Pompidou was disturbed by the loud cry of their next-door neighbour's baby and said to her husband, "If that baby is going to cry like that …"

Her husband interrupted her, "I am sure it will be a lovely baby, even if its parents are the Smiths!"

The baby was big, much bigger than any baby anybody had ever seen, and everybody in First End came to see it. Well, almost everybody, because some families had heard that the baby was 'too big' and believed that a 'too big' baby is a bad omen for the village, and Mrs Pompidou said to her husband that a huge baby was no less grotesque than a huge tummy and both should be hidden away rather than put on show.

The baby was a boy, and Mr & Mrs Smith named it Samuel.

Baby Samuel, in addition to being very big, was very healthy and had a big appetite. Even though Mrs Smith was tired and weak after the birth, she had to work hard to look after Baby Samuel.

CHAPTER V

Baby Samuel grew quickly. Much more quickly than any other baby.

One month after it was born Baby Samuel was so big that nobody could carry him anymore. That was a shock to Mrs Smith because, how can you take care of your baby if you cannot carry it? But Baby Samuel was not like other babies and although it still could not stand or walk, it already could crawl all-round the house and would crawl out to the garden if the front door was open!

So Mrs Smith had to chase after Baby Samuel to feed him and to change him, and Mr & Mrs Smith had to stay home to look after him because they could not carry him anywhere!

And what was Mrs Smith to do with all the clothes that she had prepared, the baby carriage that was useless and the cot that was too small for the new baby?

Well, Baby Samuel was far too big for any of it, and the things he needed were very different from all that Mr & Mrs Smith had prepared for him. Everybody in First End felt sorry for the Smiths. Well, almost everybody, because some people were worried about how big already Baby Samuel was, and Mrs Pompidou remarked to her husband that the Smiths deserved blame more than sympathy because who knows what the new baby will grow up to be?

Three months after he was born, Baby Samuel was walking. He was now nearly as big as Mr Smith.

Well, this was a shock to everybody in First End and even to some people in Middle End and Mrs Pompidou was more shocked than anybody else. "Mrs Smith had no business giving birth to a baby like that … just imagine what it will be like when it is six-months-old," she said to her husband. Well, Mr Pompidou agreed entirely with his wife although he did wonder whether he shouldn't look over the fence and talk to Baby Samuel before he got to be six-months-old.

Soon after walking, Baby Samuel started to talk, and when Mr & Mrs Smith would go out walking with their baby, Baby Samuel would blink and his big blue eyes would smile sweetly at everybody. He would giggle every time somebody waved at him, and his giggle was so loud it drowned every conversation.

Mrs Smith was so proud that Baby Samuel could talk at such an early age, and everybody in First End smiled at Baby Samuel and said how clever he was. Well, almost everybody, because Mrs Pompidou said that it was really just baby talk and Baby Samuel was too big to talk like that.

Baby Samuel was so different, and not everybody liked different babies, and some people in VillageAll were getting worried and they said Baby Samuel was 'like a monster'. And this upset Mrs Smith because, she said, "Baby Samuel is just a baby, a big baby, and that is all."

Baby Samuel was getting bigger so quickly that every day he looked taller, and every day he could walk faster and talk more.

Every day people would point at Baby Samuel in The StreetAll and say how tall he had become, or how big his feet had become, or how fast he could run.

Baby Samuel was already getting taller than anybody else in VillageAll, and was talking more and more, even though he could not say many things.

Mr & Mrs Smith were rushing around trying to make everything fit Baby Samuel, because when you are so big it is not easy to walk through doors, or to sleep in a bed, or to sit on a chair. Mr Smith made a special big chair and knocked big holes in the walls to make the doors higher and wider, and Mrs Smith made a special big mattress for Baby Samuel to sleep on. But even if Baby Samuel could sit on his chair, walk through doors and sleep on his mattress, everything else was so small, useless and in his way.

The bulky arms of Baby Samuel often collided with (and rather knocked out of place) table tops and chair backs and shelves, and the big feet of Baby Samuel often bumped into (and rather knocked out altogether) table legs and chairs and low drawers and cabinets. Mr Smith said that Baby Samuel's walking around the house was a little like a moving earthquake, leaving behind it a trail of debris so you knew exactly where it struck!

Of course Baby Samuel didn't mean to cause any trouble, but what can you do when everything around you is so small?

And one day Mrs Smith's toes were rather in the way of Baby Samuel's big foot, and, well, you cannot expect a baby to mind somebody else's toes, especially a very big baby, with very big feet. Mrs Smith screamed loudly, and her arms flailed as she tried to remove her toes from underneath Baby Samuel's big foot. But poor Baby Samuel was terrified at Mrs Smith's screams and his big eyes looked down at her as he stood perfectly still. Baby Samuel was very big and was able to do a lot of things but this was a situation too complicated for his grasp, and if Mr Smith had not been nearby and come to rescue Mrs Smith, well Baby Samuel just might have stood there forever!

Mrs Smith's big toe was swollen like a melon and for weeks she could not walk properly or put on her shoes, and Mrs Smith from that day decided she would not get too close to Baby Samuel, even though she loved him very much; he was her baby after all.

And Mrs Smith had to cook huge pots of food because Baby Samuel had a big appetite. And it was no use giving him baby food because baby food was for small babies with small appetites. Even though Baby Samuel was really just a baby, he ate everything that Mrs

Smith cooked for him, even though she cooked enough for a whole family!

Baby Samuel kept growing. Soon the special tall doors were starting to look small, and the special big chair was starting to feel cramped, and the special mattress was no longer long enough and poor Baby Samuel was finding himself spending more and more time in the big garden of Number One, The StreetAll.

Well, the garden was not a bad place to be. In the garden, Baby Samuel didn't have to worry about bumping into things, or damaging things or stepping on anybody's toes.

When he was in the garden he could easily see over the fence into neighbours' gardens and houses. All the neighbours of Number One were happy to see the smiling face of Baby Samuel towering over their garden wall, and greeted him with smiles and friendly chat. Well, almost all because Mrs Pompidou once shrieked and nearly fainted when Baby Samuel's face appeared in front of her as she opened the shutters of her bedroom window.

Mrs Pompidou screamed at her husband, "You have to do something."

Mr Pompidou said, "I could not agree more but after all Baby Samuel is just a baby and, well, what can you do to a baby?" Mr Pompidou didn't tell his wife that he was already doing 'something', and the something was that he was often chatting with Baby Samuel over the fence.

Mr Pompidou was chatting to Baby Samuel because he wanted to know how Mr & Mrs Smith managed to have a baby like that, and because he secretly wished he could have a baby like that of his own. Mr Pompidou was trying to become friends with Baby Samuel and he gave him candy and chocolates every time they talked over the fence.

Mr Pompidou was not the only neighbour who felt like that. Other neighbours, especially Mr Cortez also chatted to Baby Samuel and tried to find out his secret. But although Mr Cortez was very friendly and gave Baby Samuel a lot of candy, Baby Samuel liked Mr Pompidou better because he really liked the taste of the chocolate that Mr Pompidou gave him every time they met. Baby Samuel didn't get any chocolates at home because it was all Mrs Smith could do to prepare the huge amounts of food that Baby Samuel needed every day.

CHAPTER VI

By the time Baby Samuel was six-months-old he was twice as big as anybody in VillageAll, and was *still* growing fast. He could do everything and could talk about everything.

Well, almost everything. Because there were things Baby Samuel didn't know how to do. And there were things Baby Samuel didn't understand. Baby Samuel liked to talk to his neighbours and ask them questions. He liked to talk to Mr Pompidou most.

And one day while Baby Samuel was talking with Mr Pompidou he said that although he loved Mr & Mrs Smith, because of course they were his parents, and although he liked the nice big garden of Number One, The StreetAll, he really needed a bigger place. Mr Pompidou said he had an idea.

The next day the people in First End were very surprised to see Baby Samuel busy doing something important in the big garden that used to be part of the village common, and which was now part of the Smiths' garden[32].They could see that Baby Samuel was building something. They could also see that Mr & Mrs Smith were visiting him and bringing food and other things, and that they were not the only visitors: Mr Pompidou was often with Baby Samuel, and seemed to be helping him build whatever Baby Samuel was building. Soon other people also started visiting Baby Samuel and helping him, especially Mr Cortez and Mr De Graff. After two days the people of First End could see what Baby Samuel was building: he was building a house.

A big house.

A very big house.

Well, if you are as big as Baby Samuel you need a very big house. And if you are as big as Baby Samuel you can build your own very big house. And all the people of First End were happy for Baby Samuel.

Well, almost all. Because Mr & Mrs Smith loved Baby Samuel and didn't really want him to leave their house, and Mrs Pompidou was most unhappy and said to her husband, "Why couldn't the Smiths and their baby live in a house like ours?" and her husband said he couldn't agree more, but Baby Samuel was not like his parents, Baby Samuel was not like anybody, and, who knows, if Mr & Mrs Pompidou could be friends with him he might grow up to be like them.

Baby Samuel's house was big. It covered a big part of what used to be the village common. And even if Baby Samuel was really just a baby, his new house didn't look babyish. But although Baby Samuel's house was not babyish it was not like grown-up houses either; Baby Samuel was big and strong and could build big walls and rooms with very high ceilings and very tall doors but, well, he was just a baby and it was difficult for him to make the walls straight and upright, and to make the ceiling level, and to make the windows the same size or shape ... well Baby Samuel didn't think it mattered at all because all he wanted was a place big enough to live in!

Baby Samuel built his house very quickly, much more quickly than a whole lot of men working together, because Baby Samuel could move so quickly, could carry big and heavy loads and didn't need to rest often. And although both Mr Cortez and Mr Pompidou at first tried to help Baby Samuel and bring him stuff for his house, they soon realised that it was very difficult to help Baby Samuel because he was very different and did everything very differently!

As the house was taking shape, everybody in First End said how unusual and how interesting it was going to be. Well, almost everybody, because Mrs Pompidou, although impressed by the size and height of the house, said it looked awful and Baby Samuel really had better listen to Mr Pompidou's ideas about how to make it look better.

The finished house looked like a giant's house, well, actually more like a crooked giant's house, towering over all other houses in VillageAll. And it soon became a very big feature of VillageAll, since it could be seen from the two ends of the village and especially the people of First End could see it from their own houses. The people of Middle End could see it from a distance but didn't want to go near it because they said they didn't know if the 'giant baby' was friendly or not, and the people of Far End, well, they were far and they said they were not bothered by what people did in First End, even if they had giant babies who built giant houses!

Baby Samuel was rather pleased with himself because he now had a place of his own which was big enough for him to live the way he wanted to, and to do the things he wanted to do.

Even if the house was not very comfortable or very elegant, Baby Samuel had so much energy and strength that it was easy for him to make his house better all the time. And, well, Baby Samuel was still growing fast, so he had to keep making his house bigger …

One day soon after Baby Samuel finished building his house, a group of Nomans appeared suddenly. They walked by the river and climbed up the bank to the big field, which was the village common, and as they stepped on to the common they raised their heads and then stood and stared at the giant new house. Of course nobody in First End took much notice, and Baby Samuel was busy in his new house and although he did glimpse the Nomans he didn't think it had anything to do with him. Well, he was just a baby and babies don't worry about other people and what they want, especially if these people were the Nomans.

CHAPTER VII

Even though Mrs Smith was working very hard to make lots and lots of food for Baby Samuel, he was hungry most of the time. Well, a giant baby has a giant appetite and a giant baby needs giant meals!

Although Baby Samuel was just a baby, his appetite gave him many ideas about how and where to get food. And although Baby Samuel was just a baby, because he was so much bigger than anybody in VillageAll he could do things and go to places nobody had thought of before.

Soon, Baby Samuel was wading into the river to catch lots and lots of fish, which became big meals that satisfied his hunger. It was not long after that he ventured across the river to the opposite bank. Baby Samuel was so big that he could walk on the riverbed and in the deepest part the water came up only to his shoulders. When he climbed up the opposite bank he could see fields, which stretched endlessly. He became excited when he realised that the fields and meadows in front of him didn't have any people or houses or roads so he could walk and run and frolic without fear of bumping into anything or anybody, or being told he was noisy, or to be careful, or, or …

But Baby Samuel was not the only one excited. Everybody, including Mrs Pompidou, looked in awe and wonder as Baby Samuel first waded into the river to catch fish, and then later as he crossed the river and climbed up the opposite bank. Nobody in all of VillageAll had ever seen anything like that!

Soon, Baby Samuel was spending every day on the other side of the river, exploring further and further afield, and returning home with game and other animals that he found in abundance in the fields far away from VillageAll.

Baby Samuel now had plenty to eat, and Mrs Smith no longer cooked for him.

And although Baby Samuel was just a baby, he now had many friends in First End because many people wanted to know about the faraway places that Baby Samuel went to.

While Baby Samuel was busy with his explorations in the faraway places, First End became abuzz with the news that Mr Pompidou had decided he would no longer agree with his wife[33] about everything! Well, that was big news because although everybody now knew what Mr Pompidou would *not* agree with, nobody yet knew what Mr Pompidou *would* agree with. And although not everybody liked Mrs Pompidou, everybody agreed that Mr Pompidou and Mrs Pompidou upsetting each other was much worse than anybody upsetting either or both!

But Mr Pompidou looked cheerful and happy. So everybody relaxed and smiled at him. Well, almost everybody, because Mrs Pompidou didn't relax, and was not smiling at anybody.

Mr Pompidou searched out Baby Samuel to tell him the news. But Mr Pompidou wanted to keep such a big friend as Baby Samuel, because Mr Pompidou knew that not agreeing with his wife didn't mean agreeing with anybody or agreeing with everybody. Well, Baby Samuel listened to the news but said nothing. He liked Mr Pompidou and wanted to be friends with him but didn't really understand if the news meant he could catch more food or not, or if he could spend more or less time on the other side of the river ...Baby Samuel had no other thoughts on his mind. Baby Samuel only cheered up when Mr Pompidou told him that because he decided not to agree with Mrs Pompidou anymore, he could help him catch more fish and teach him how to trap more and better game for his meals.

Mr Pompidou soon found that not agreeing with his wife made him the most important man in First End[34,] because everybody wanted to be friends with him. Well, almost everybody, because Mr & Mrs Smith didn't want to be friends with him anymore. Mr Smith was angry because he was no longer the most important man in First End. Mr & Mrs Smith were also angry because they didn't want Baby Samuel to be friends with Mr Pompidou, because Baby Samuel was not just a baby, he was *their* baby. Mrs Smith was not only angry but was also worried because she thought: *What if Mr Smith decided to do the same as Mr Pompidou and stopped agreeing with her?*

Well, First End was awash with excitement, and a bit of confusion, about who would agree with whom, and who would not agree with whom.

But not only First End. Because both Mr Pompidou and Mr Smith also had friends in Middle End, and even knew some people in Far End. And their friends in Middle End and Far End now shared in the excitement, and confusion, about who agreed with whom.

But especially Mr Singh, because he wanted to know if he should be friends with Mr Smith or with Mr Pompidou. Mr Singh worked very hard to take care of his large family. Every day he was tired and harassed. He wanted to be relaxed and happy, and maybe a little more important, like Mr Pompidou, who no longer agreed with his wife. But Mrs Singh was also tired and harassed. So when Mr Singh, like Mr Pompidou, no longer agreed with Mrs Singh, he was surprised to find that, unlike Mr Pompidou, he became even more tired and harassed, and didn't become one bit more important!

Well, that settled it for Mr Singh: he decided that it was Mr Smith he wanted to be friends with! [35]

Mr Smith soon told everybody in First End, and it was big news. And Mr Pompidou was now unhappy because he worried that many of his new friends would do what Mr Singh did. So Mr Pompidou decided to talk to Baby Samuel again.

Mr Pompidou showed Baby Samuel how to make special traps for catching more animals for his meals. Mr Pompidou helped Baby Samuel make one of the special traps, which hangs on a tree. Baby Samuel hung the trap on a nail in the wall.

Although the nail was only at Baby Samuel's shoulder height, it was considerably higher than Mr Smith's head, and, well, the floors and walls of the giant house were neither straight nor firm, especially when Baby Samuel was leaping up-or-downstairs in his peculiar impatient, halting way. It was not Baby Samuel's fault that Mr Smith happened to be precisely under the trap when Baby Samuel was careering downstairs ... The trap shook free from its nail and fell down straight on Mr Smith's nose and pinched it so fiercely that both Mr Smith and Baby Samuel thought they would never find Mr Smith's nose again[36]. But Mr Smith's nose held firm and the trap dangled down from his head swinging like a mangled pendulum. Mr Smith's nose was quite bloody, and so was his temper. Mr Smith told Baby Samuel he was not to speak to Mr Pompidou ever again. Although Baby Samuel liked Mr Pompidou and wanted to speak to him again, he didn't like to give Mr Smith a bloody nose, or a bloody temper. Baby Samuel was still a baby, after all.

Everybody in First End felt sorry for Mr Smith's bloody nose, and even sorrier for his bloody temper. Well, almost everybody, because some people thought Mr Smith deserved a bloody nose, and Mr Pompidou said to his wife that Mr Smith was a big bully anyway, and Mrs Pompidou said she could not agree more.

"Did you hear that?" whispered all the ladies of First End. Because Mrs Pompidou agreeing with her husband was very big news indeed!

Mr & Mrs Cortez felt sorry neither for Mr Smith nor for Mr Pompidou. They mostly felt sorry for themselves. Well, it is not easy to have so many relatives in a small house, and the neighbours heard their quarrels every day. Finally, Mr & Mrs Cortez gave most of their big garden to their relatives to build their own houses. The Cortez family could only keep for themselves a very small garden, which was strange because they once had the biggest garden of all[37].

The Smiths not only had the biggest garden now, but also had more friends and in more places than anybody else. Mr Smith often went to Far End, and was invited to tea at the Aungs' and at the Chens'. And although neither the Aungs nor the Chens were invited to tea at the Smiths', both families were happy to invite Mr Smith again and again. Well, the Smiths after all had the biggest house and biggest garden in VillageAll and could not be expected to invite everybody to tea!

CHAPTER VIII

One day, Baby Samuel was woken very early in the morning by the sound of crying babies. Even though Baby Samuel was just a baby he was a giant baby, and giant babies don't cry. Baby Samuel hadn't cried since the enormous shriek he gave when he was born. Baby Samuel didn't like hearing babies cry because it gave him a bad headache. So Baby Samuel always ran away from crying babies.

But this time Baby Samuel thought the crying was coming from his kitchen, and, well, you cannot run away from your own kitchen, especially when you were sleepy and had not yet had your breakfast.

Baby Samuel, with eyes half shut, and head aching, stumbled in the direction of the noise. A large group of Nomans had come up the riverbank and camped just outside Baby Samuel's kitchen window. They were busy cooking the fish they caught. Babies were crying and children were running around and making a racket.

As the noise grew so Baby Samuel's headache got worse and when he burst out of the door of the kitchen and saw the Nomans he sighed out loudly, which to the Nomans came out like a loud growl, and raised his arms and waved them towards the river to tell the Nomans to go away. What the Nomans saw was a giant about to pounce on them and tear them to pieces. For an instant they froze with terror, and then it was pandemonium … they were running in all directions, falling over each other, in the fire, and in the river. The few who survived fled down the riverbank where they came from. Babies, children, and many men and women had fallen in the river and were swept away by the fast currents[38].

Baby Samuel opened his eyes to a sight of total destruction, with not one Noman remaining. Baby Samuel no longer had a headache because there were no more babies crying. Those Noman babies would never cry again.

Baby Samuel didn't want the Nomans to drown, but it was not his fault that they gave him a headache and then were frightened of him. Well, he was just a baby and babies don't worry about other people and what they are frightened of.

Of course nobody in First End took much notice. Baby Samuel had to take care of his house, and people had better not upset him, especially if these people were the Nomans.

CHAPTER IX

Even though Baby Samuel was already a huge baby, he was still growing fast. But the house he built, which was also huge, was not growing fast, or slowly, or even at all. So, one day Baby Samuel started to build a much bigger house, using all the rest of what used to be the village common[39].

Everybody in First End was pleased for Baby Samuel because now he would have a better and bigger house. Well, almost everybody, because some people said it would be a pity to lose all the village common, even though it was no longer the village common, and especially the Cortez family, who still owned a bit of what used to be the old common, and was growing almost as fast as Baby Samuel and wanted to use their bit for an aunt or an uncle to build a house on.

Well, the Smiths of course said they were happy to give their big garden to Baby Samuel, and Mr Pompidou wanted to keep Baby Samuel as his friend, so he also said he was happy to give up his bit of what used to be the village common (and Mrs Pompidou said she couldn't agree more)! Well, what could the Cortez family do but pretend to be happy to give up their bit of what used to be the village common?

While everybody was telling everybody how happy or unhappy they were about giving up what used to be the village common, Baby Samuel was busy building his bigger home. Baby Samuel had no idea what everybody was saying and, really, didn't care to know. Well, he was a baby after all, and babies know what they want; they do not care what other people say or think.

Soon Baby Samuel finished building his new house and then demolished the old one. The new house, although much bigger than the old one, still had some space to grow into if Baby Samuel grew much bigger, and Baby Samuel looked every bit as if he was going to!

As the new house now occupied more of what used to be the village common, it was closer to Middle End and Far End. Baby Samuel now met with people from Middle End and sometimes walked over to have a look around Far End.

Although Baby Samuel was, like other babies, quite curious, he didn't know much about other people. He just wanted to have enough to eat, which was not always easy because although there was plenty of fish in the river and game on the other side, Baby Samuel wanted also to eat bread and vegetables and sometimes wanted to eat bacon and beef and other times wanted to drink milk and eat butter and cheese. So Baby Samuel started to go regularly to the First End bakery and grocer, and sometimes to the First End butcher and dairy shop. The

First End shops liked a giant customer with a giant appetite, and their businesses started to get bigger.

And Baby Samuel wanted enough big space to run around freely, which was only possible on the other side of the river. So Baby Samuel didn't notice some things happening in VillageAll, and could not help when people had quarrels, like the quarrels of Mr Osman and Mr Popov, which were still going on, especially after Mr Popov one day took away Mr Osman's water pipe, when Mr Osman was inside his house[40]. At that time Mr Osman was good friends with Mr Smith and asked for his help. Well, Mr Smith wanted to help Mr Osman but he was worried because he didn't know Mr Popov and because Mr Popov was a big man. So Mr Smith had an idea: he would ask Mr Pompidou to go with him, because Mr Pompidou knew Mr Popov, and because Mr Smith wanted to make amends with Mr Pompidou since Mr Smith was once again the most important man in First End. So Mr Smith and Mr Pompidou went together to see Mr Popov. And although Mr Popov was big, he was not big enough to upset both Mr Smith and Mr Pompidou, so he gave them Mr Osman's water pipe and promised not to take it again.

CHAPTER X

Although Baby Samuel didn't notice many of the things happening in VillageAll, one day when he was walking in Far End he did notice the Watanabes' house. Baby Samuel stood in front of the long, high white wall and thought there was something very strange. There was a sign with the name of Mr & Mrs Watanabe. But, but … there was no door!

"There is no door," Baby Samuel kept repeating to himself. Because, although Baby Samuel was just a baby and didn't worry about other people and what they did, there were things which bothered him very much. And a house with no front door was one of those things. Baby Samuel stood staring at the white wall with no door, repeating, very loudly now, "There is no door," his voice reverberating up and down The StreetAll so people passing by felt they had better go somewhere else. Suddenly Baby Samuel gathered both fists, raised his long and powerful arms high above his head and brought his fists down on the wall with a huge thump. Although he was just a baby, Baby Samuel was a giant baby, and giant fists can cause a lot of damage to a white wall with no door! Well, the wall crumpled where the fists hit and a large chunk fell into the Watanabes' garden-in-house, making a big opening in the wall[41].

When Baby Samuel had started his 'there is no door' chanting, Mrs Watanabe inside the house was the first to hear him. She said to her husband there was a strange sound coming from the street. Mr Watanabe strained to hear; his hearing was waning with age and some sounds he hardly heard at all, while other sounds he heard loudly. By the time Mr Watanabe could hear the noise, Mrs Watanabe said it was somebody's voice, strange voice as it was, and was getting louder and more menacing. Mr Watanabe on hearing this, rose with a jump, rearranged his kimono, grabbed his two samurai swords, the short one and the long one, and wore them ready for action, and started towards the door. But Mrs Watanabe was quicker and moved in front of him to stop his abrupt rush. Mrs Watanabe said to her husband that he had better be careful because she had heard that there were 'giants' in other parts of VillageAll. Of course the Watanabes didn't know very much about VillageAll, nor, of course, did VillageAll know much about the Watanabes. And stories about giants could be very scary if you didn't know very much.

Mr Watanabe was still determined to go out to the garden to investigate. And even though he put on a very fierce look and marched forward with an exaggerated swagger, he was, inside, trembling with fear as Baby Samuel's voice finally reached him. He had just stepped out on to the veranda, with his wife close behind, when Baby Samuel's fists landed on the wall. The sound of the crashing wall happened to be one of the sounds that Mr Watanabe's aging ears heard extremely loudly, so the sound came to him as a bolt of thunder. The shock buckled Mr Watanabe's knees and he fell backwards into his wife's arms. Mrs Watanabe staggered backwards under her husband's weight but stayed up, and then helped her husband back to his trembling feet as they both looked at the debris settling on the ground and the dust clearing to reveal the gaping hole in the wall. Mr Watanabe was now reluctant to go anywhere, two samurai swords in his belt notwithstanding, but his wife pushed him forward and together they cautiously advanced toward the wall.

Baby Samuel, meanwhile, had calmed down. And although the gap he made in the wall didn't look much like a front door, he felt much happier, and when he glimpsed through the ragged edges of the gap the whitened, stiff face of Mr Watanabe, and the slightly shaken, slightly angry but more determined face of Mrs Watanabe, he smiled at them and pointed to the gap.

Well, it seems the Watanabes got the message. Because the very next day Mr Watanabe announced that there would be a ceremony of the Grand Door, when a grand front door would be installed in the Watanabes' long white wall with no door. Many people from First End were invited to the ceremony because, of course, Baby Samuel was from First End. The ceremony was duly held, and the front door was installed.

Well, doors are for opening, and Mr & Mrs Watanabe soon discovered that a front door to their house was also a front door to the street, and to the people in the street, and to VillageAll. And that terrified Mr & Mrs Watanabe. Well, the Watanabes didn't know very much about VillageAll, and thought: *What if they found in VillageAll somebody or something they did not like*? and *What if somebody or something in VillageAll did not like them?* and *What if the somebody or something they did not like, or the somebody or something that did not like them, knocked on their door?*

Well, what could the Watanabes do? They now had a grand front door, and in First End there was a giant baby with giant fists.

Of course the Watanabes soon found that VillageAll was neither full of giants, nor full of people they didn't like, nor of people who didn't like them. They started to meet many people and to make friends. They already knew a few families in Far End, and long, long ago had met the De Graff and Cortez families, and now met many more families from First End. But although Mr Watanabe walked many times between Far End and First End, he always hurried past Middle End and never met anybody in Middle End! Even though Mr Watanabe always hurried past Middle End he was always careful not to tread on the Ndiayes' flowers and bushes, as people from First End always did, and as people from Far End never did.

Mr Smith was the first of First End people who met the Watanabes. Well, of course Baby Samuel was first, but he was just a baby, even if he was a baby who could knock a big hole in a wall with no door, and well, Mr &

53

Mrs Watanabe didn't feel they really *met* Baby Samuel at all!

Mr Smith now often visited his friends in Far End, and found the idea of knocking on the Watanabes' now famous new front door quite exciting. Mr Smith had heard from his friends in Far End that the Watanabes had a very beautiful garden-in-house and, well, Mr Smith was not only a smith, but also a gardener, and a First End gardener had to see all the best gardens, so he could explain why his garden was the very best!

CHAPTER XI

Around the time of the Watanabes' front door event, Mr Smith wanted to become more friendly with the Chens because he heard that they had a lot of food in their big house and he wanted to get some of the food to First End. Mr Smith sent a messenger to the Chens with gifts which he had got from Mr Singh. Although Mrs Chen was happy to get the gifts from an important person, such as Mr Smith, Mr Chen said the gifts were bad for the Chens because First End people only gave gifts when they wanted back ten times more gifts, so he sent them back with the messenger[42].

Soon after that incident the whole Chen family became very poorly, and continued to be poorly for a long time[43].

In the meantime, Mr Smith, who thought that maybe the Chens didn't know he was such an important person in VillageAll, decided that this time he would go by himself and take the same gifts again. Mr Smith was so important that he thought everybody would be so pleased to see him, so he never asked before visiting, and just turned up at the Chens'. Well, the Chens were all so poorly that when Mr Smith knocked on the door nobody came to open the door for him as everybody inside was poorly in bed. Mr Smith was somewhat puzzled, and a little annoyed and a little angry with Mr Chen, and became even more sure that the Chens didn't know of his importance[44].

Mr Smith decided he would come back to visit again and that time he would make sure Mr Chen knew, and would make sure to finish his business with the Chens. But Mr Smith heard that the Chens continued to be poorly and he heard from his friends in First End that, more than visitors from First End, what the Chens needed most was some medicine to make them better.

Soon after he heard that, Mr Smith and some of his friends from First End took medicine to the Chens, and this time didn't insist to visit with them.

Although the Chens started to feel better after taking the medicine, it was a very long time before they recovered. Mr Chen said that they needed more of Mr Smith's medicine, but Mrs Chen said that they needed more Far End medicine and that Mr Smith's medicine would make Mr Chen ill again.

Although Mr Smith offered medicine to the Chens, Mr Smith, and everybody else in First End were soon very ill and had no medicine for their illness[45].

Baby Samuel was the first to catch the illness. He felt dizzy and weak. Baby Samuel told Mrs Smith he didn't feel well, and that day stayed home. Mrs Smith then visited Baby Samuel and took some food for him. And when Mr Pompidou heard, he also visited Baby

Samuel to wish him well. But soon the Smiths and the Pompidous were also ill. And soon everybody in First End was ill. Everybody in First End was frightened, even Mr & Mrs Pompidou, because it was the first time ever that everybody in First End was ill at the same time, and because it was a new illness nobody had a medicine for.

Although nobody died in First End, many people didn't have anything to eat for many, many days, and Baby Samuel stayed home for two whole days, which was unheard of! And although Mr Smith said he had heard that the First End chemist had found a medicine for the new illness, nobody had seen the medicine and nobody knew what to do if the new illness came back again.

But some people in First End said they saw Mr Smith talking to Knabers[46]. They said Knabers brought food to him and to Baby Samuel. Well, people can say anything about Knabers because nobody knew anything about them! But some people say they have seen them. They say Knabers were small and had very strange faces and didn't talk to anybody. There were rumours in VillageAll about how Knabers came from KnabLand, and everybody said KnabLand was too far away to reach. Well, almost everybody, because some people said the Knabers really lived in holes in the ground in the Smiths' garden, and they only came out at night so nobody could see them.

The people who lived in First End didn't like little strange people who lived in holes, and Mrs Pompidou said to her husband, "Maybe the Knabers brought the illness to everybody in First End."

Mr Pompidou said, "If the Knabers brought the illness then maybe the Knabers also have the medicine."

CHAPTER XII

Baby Samuel was now nearly one-year-old. He was now towering over everybody and everything, because Baby Samuel was now almost three times as big as anybody in VillageAll. His new house already needed to grow again to catch up with him.

And Baby Samuel was still growing fast. So, although Baby Samuel was just a baby, and he just liked to cross the river to enjoy open space on the other side, everybody in First End looked over their shoulder when they passed his house, to see if he was there, to see what he was doing, and to see how big he had become.

"It is not easy to live with a giant," said Mrs Schmidt.

"How big will Baby Samuel be?" said Mrs Cortez.

"Will Baby Samuel ever grow up?" asked Mrs De Graff.

But Mrs Pompidou, who now agreed with Mr Pompidou, said Baby Samuel was just a nice baby and there was nothing to worry about.

Two weeks before his first birthday, Baby Samuel looked happy and had a big smile. He was walking to the Smiths' house waving a bundle of flowers in his hand;

they were a funny collection of many shapes and colours, some with short stems and some with long ones.

Baby Samuel was waving the flowers at everybody he passed and saying, with his booming baby voice, "Flowers for Mrs Smith."

Well, Mrs Smith was very pleased with the flowers. But when Baby Samuel told her he picked the flowers from the bushes in front of Mr & Mrs Ndiaye's house, Mrs Smith was not happy anymore. Mrs Smith said that the flowers belonged to the Ndiayes, and did Baby Samuel ask if he could have them?

"No," said Baby Samuel, "because the Ndiayes' garden has no wall or fence so nothing belongs to them and I can take flowers whenever I want."

Well, Mrs Smith was rather cross with Baby Samuel and said that he was never to take flowers again from in front of the Ndiayes' house. Baby Samuel felt ashamed and felt bad and left Mrs Smith in a sulky mood. He walked off to the riverbank and then, still feeling bad, he gave the trunk of a tree a very hard kick. Although the tree was quite big it only came up to Baby Samuel's shoulders. The tree was a needle pine tree with a thick trunk, which Baby Samuel could not see from his height, and only realised from the sharp pain in his toes how thick it was. As Baby Samuel bent down from the pain, the tree bent back after the kick straight into Baby Samuel's face, the needles scratching and cutting his face. Baby Samuel screamed in pain and clutched at his face and then hurried back to his home in an even sulkier mood[47].

Although Baby Samuel remained in a sulky mood for some days he learnt to be careful with all flowers in future. Well, almost all flowers because Baby Samuel thought that there were still many flowers that belonged to nobody, for how could a baby know when flowers belonged to anybody?

Baby Samuel told everybody in First End that he was going to have a big birthday party and asked them to come. And in the weeks before his first birthday, Baby Samuel spent more and more time away on the other side of the river. He would leave very early in the morning and come back home late, carrying food and stuff for building and making things.

On the day of his birthday Baby Samuel spent the morning building new rooms for his house, with higher ceilings and larger windows and doors. Baby Samuel thought that it would not do to have his birthday party in cramped rooms with low ceilings and small doors. Of course Baby Samuel's visitors were already dwarfed by his house and didn't feel either that the rooms were cramped or that the ceilings were low! But Baby Samuel was just a baby and babies only know what they feel and see.

Many people from First End came to Baby Samuel's birthday party. Baby Samuel had prepared a lot of food and some soft drinks (well, babies don't drink anything else). There was plenty for everybody to eat, and although some of the food was unusual, because it came from unusual places, and everybody said it tasted good, a lot of the other food didn't look good, and didn't taste any better. Well, Baby Samuel was not a cook, and for a giant baby finding *enough* food was more important than finding tasty food.

At the end of the party Baby Samuel told everybody that his house would no longer be in First End but would now be in New End, and that New End would include all the places Baby Samuel found on the other side of the river. Baby Samuel also told everybody that he could now reach very far on the other side of the river, all the way to another big river, because he had now grown big enough to run far and jump over bushes, rocks and ravines. Well, everybody was impressed and wished they too would be big enough to go to new interesting places like Baby Samuel did. Well, almost everybody, because although Mr & Mrs Smith were impressed like everybody else, they had no wish to either be big or to go to faraway places since they felt that one giant member in the family is quite enough, and had no wish to do the things that Baby Samuel did.

But even though Mr & Mrs Smith still felt they were family with their giant baby, Baby Samuel, although only one-year-old, felt so big and wanted to do his own 'big baby' things that he no longer felt Mr & Mrs Smith were family, but rather close friends, perhaps a little more special than his other close friends.

CHAPTER XIII

Although Mr & Mrs Watanabe were not invited to Baby Samuel's birthday party, they heard about it from their friends in First End, and it gave them the idea of having a garden party for the friends they made after their house became like other houses, a house with a front door.

The Watanabes invited all their friends from First End, including Baby Samuel, and also some of their neighbours in Far End. But although the Kims were quite close to the Watanabes, they were not invited because Mr & Mrs Chen said that the Kims were too poor and shouldn't be invited, and the Watanabes didn't want to upset Mr & Mrs Chen.

The Watanabes' garden party[48] was successful and everybody liked the garden-in-house and enjoyed the special tea, which only Mrs Watanabe knew how to prepare. Baby Samuel was too big to sit on a normal chair so he sat on the ground beside Mr & Mrs Smith and was rather quiet. Well, he was just a baby and babies don't like other people's parties.

Mr Watanabe told everybody during the party that as his family was getting bigger, he was going to build new rooms in his house. Mr Watanabe now not only liked houses with front doors, but also liked the colours and styles of houses in First End, so he told his guests that his friends from First End will help to design the new rooms for his family.

Although Mr & Mrs Watanabe were very pleased with how their garden party went, Mrs Watanabe was unhappy that they had listened to the Chens and had not invited the Kims.

The Kims were a very quiet family and didn't want to make trouble with the Chens either. Although Mr & Mrs Kim remained friendly with the Watanabes, Mrs Watanabe decided to have a special party for the Kims to which she decided not to invite Mr & Mrs Chen.

When the Kims received the invitation they were a little worried about upsetting Mr & Mrs Chen, but then Mrs Watanabe herself visited them and said they must come and that Mr & Mrs Watanabe would make sure the Chens didn't make any trouble. The Watanabes had invited only a few friends and the party was again a success[49].

The Chens, meanwhile, were more worried about their quarrel with Mr Pompidou[50] than about the Watanabes' party for the Kims. Mr Pompidou was visiting their neighbours, Mr & Mrs Phong, and telling them their tea tasted much better than the Chens'. Well, this was very serious indeed and Mrs Chen said to her husband that if he didn't do something immediately she was going to take things into her own hands. Mr Chen knew that whether or not he agreed with his wife, it was not a good idea to let her take things into her own hands. So Mr Chen went to visit Mr Pompidou and had a long chat with him about tea and First End and Far End, and the Chens and finally Mr Pompidou agreed that Mrs Chen's tea was quite delicious and the two were friends again.

Mr Pompidou had another thing on his mind, besides the matter of Mrs Chen's tea. Because Mr Pompidou felt that although he and Mrs Pompidou celebrated Baby Samuel's birthday with him, Mr Pompidou wanted to give Baby Samuel a present for such an important occasion (a big present, seeing how big Baby Samuel had become!)

Mrs Pompidou, although she would now agree with her husband, said, "But what kind of a big present would Baby Samuel want?" Mr Pompidou said he wanted Baby Samuel to feel that the Pompidous were his best friends, and wanted everybody in First End to see that they were. Well, almost everybody, because Mr & Mrs Smith neither wanted to see, nor wanted Baby Samuel to feel that the Pompidous were his best friends!

Mrs Pompidou remembered that Baby Samuel's house didn't have any pictures, and thought that he would like to hang a picture on the wall of his living room so he would always see it and think of the Pompidous. Mr Pompidou thought it was a very good idea, especially because he would not have to do anything. Well, you see, Mrs Pompidou was not only famous for her loud singing, but also famous for the very bright, colourful pictures which she painted. But although Mrs Pompidou had painted many pictures for her friends' houses, she had never painted a giant picture for a giant's house.

When Mrs Pompidou had prepared the frame and canvas of the giant picture she looked worried and said to her husband, "Look how big this picture is! How am I going to find enough trees, and rivers, and horses, and flowers and skies and clouds to fill it up?"

Mrs Pompidou worked very hard over many days and weeks and when she finally finished the painting it was not only the biggest painting she had ever painted, but one of her brightest and most colourful, even if it was not one of her best! Well, Baby Samuel was just a baby, and babies liked big, bright and colourful pictures most, and so was very excited when the Pompidous delivered the picture to his house. The picture was so big and heavy that Baby Samuel built a special frame and made the wall stronger so he could hang it safely. After that Baby Samuel invited everybody in First End to come to his house to see the picture. Many of Baby Samuel's friends came and admired the picture and said how clever Mrs Pompidou was, even though nobody could quite see the picture as, of course, it was hanging far above their heads[51].

Baby Samuel was very pleased with his new picture and felt that it made him important because nobody else in First End had such a big, bright and colourful picture.

One day, soon after Baby Samuel got the picture, he was returning home early in the morning after a trip to the bakery, when he saw a movement at the back of his house and then realised that two Noman kids were entering his kitchen through the back door. Baby Samuel's mind was still so full of his picture and how important it made him that he could not think of anything else. So when he saw the Noman kids getting into his house he was convinced they would steal or ruin his precious picture, and he was very, very angry.

Baby Samuel rushed to his house, flung the enormous load of bread loaves and buns on the floor and went straight to the kitchen. At the kitchen door he met with the two kids as they were heading out of the kitchen and into the living room. Baby Samuel grabbed the two kids with one hand and lifted them up in the air as he walked through the kitchen. Before Baby Samuel could reach the back door it burst open and a few Nomans came in shouting and waving their arms, and at the same time the two kids he was holding started crying with a shriek. The crying made Baby Samuel's head ache so he grabbed all the Nomans, walked over to the veranda overhanging the river, and flung them all far into the river[52].

The Nomans disappeared in the rushing waters, and nobody ever heard of them again.

Of course nobody in First End took much notice. Baby Samuel had to take care of his picture, and people had better not upset him, especially if these people were the Nomans.

CHAPTER XIV

Although Mr & Mrs Watanabe made many friends after the Grand Front Door ceremony, they now found that although VillageAll was neither full of giants, nor full of people they didn't like, nor of people who didn't like them, VillageAll was also neither full of people who did like them, or of people they did like!

The Chens lived next door to the Watanabes on one side, and the two families shared a garden wall at the back of their gardens. The Chens had a fruit tree right at the back of their garden, by that wall, and as the tree grew taller and wider, some branches hung more and more over the Watanabes' garden.

One day Mrs Watanabe was walking in her garden when she noticed the branches of the tree hanging over her garden. The branches were bending down low because of the weight of the fruit, which looked delicious, so Mrs Watanabe picked a load of the fruit and took it in the house to eat with her husband[53].

Mrs Watanabe didn't see Mrs Chen, who stood quite close to the tree watching while Mrs Watanabe picked the fruit, and Mrs Watanabe didn't know that Mrs Chen didn't like to see the Watanabes picking fruit from her tree.

The Chens and Watanabes had a big quarrel over the fruit tree, and although after some time, friends from First End helped them to end their quarrel, as the tree remained, and continued to grow bigger and wider, the Chens and Watanabes didn't become friends again.

But the Watanabes had more quarrels.

Mr Watanabe sometimes walked to First End using the back streets and paths in the countryside behind the houses of VillageAll. Mr Watanabe's route took him by the Popovs' house. Although not many people used this route, Mr Watanabe liked to use it from time to time because he said sometimes it was good to walk without meeting other people, and also that walking the back route he could see how some of the houses far away from The StreetAll were changing and what people did with their back gardens.

One day Mr Watanabe decided to go to First End using this route. But as he got near the Popov house he could see an obstacle ahead of him. As he got nearer he saw that his path was blocked by a new construction extending from the Popov house. It seemed that Mr Popov had decided to extend his garden and build a new shed into the path.

Mr Watanabe was very upset and knocked on the Popovs' door and when Mr Popov opened the door shouted angrily at him[54]. Well, Mr Popov was a big man and didn't often get shouted at, especially not angrily, so

Mr Popov also felt angry and his face became even redder than usual. But although Mr Watanabe was not as big as him, Mr Popov suddenly noticed the two menacing swords in Mr Watanabe's belt, so instead of stepping forward with fists raised, Mr Popov gave a big hearty laugh, so as to say there was no quarrel amongst friends, and said he would remove the new shed immediately. Mr Watanabe's path was clear again, and the quarrel was over.

People in First End and Far End talked about Mr Watanabe's quarrel with Mr Popov and said that if Mr Watanabe could stand up to Mr Popov then he was quite an important person in VillageAll, and so many people wanted to be friends with the Watanabes.

Soon after the quarrels of the Watanabes, the men in First End got together and started a 'Men's Club', which was mainly for betting and gambling and other things that men do, which sometimes other people don't like. Because Mr Watanabe now had many friends in First End, he was allowed to become a member. Baby Samuel, who now lived in New End, also became a member. Although Baby Samuel was just a baby, and babies don't become members of men's clubs, all members of the new club wanted Baby Samuel to be a member, because he was so handy with many things, and also because he had recently started selling fish and game to First End shops and now had a lot of food.

The 'Men's Club' became famous in VillageAll because all the most important people were members, and because members had a good time and agreed on many things to do or not to do in VillageAll. Although the men always gambled on club nights, they only gambled for fun and only lost (mostly) or won a little, which didn't change anything in VillageAll.

But one night, the members of the club were very excited and decided they would make big bets, very big bets, very, very big bets …

And that was a famous night in VillageAll[55].

Because if you make very, very big bets then you lose very, very big.

And that night almost everybody in First End lost very, very big. The biggest winners were Mr Smith and Mr Pompidou. Baby Samuel, who didn't know about betting and gambling just did what Mr Smith and Mr Pompidou did, and so also won that night.

Well, after that famous night nobody went to the Men's Club for a long time, and many families in First End were poor and had to live in smaller houses or have smaller gardens.

People in First End didn't feel good anymore and everybody said how good the old times were before the men of First End lost their minds in their 'Men's Club'.

But, well, for Mr Smith and Mr Pompidou it was different, because they both became the most important men in VillageAll, even if they were not the most popular, especially in First End. They now had more friends in Middle End and, especially Mr Smith, now had many more friends in Far End.

Although Mr Popov was not a big loser, he had used his family's money and now all his family quarrelled with him and didn't agree with him anymore[56]. Mr Popov went to stay with his friends who lived close by, and told them that it was all Baby Samuel's fault that he lost his family's money. Well, Mr Popov's friends liked him and they thought that Baby Samuel did something terrible to their friend. Mr Popov, who very much wanted to go back to his family and his house, agreed with his friends to start a special club to tell everybody in VillageAll how bad Baby Samuel was. They called their club the 'Unique Side Show Ring'[57] because they were going to make a side show to every show that Baby Samuel made.

Although not many people joined the special club, it became famous in VillageAll, and many people from Middle End and Far End talked to Mr Popov and wanted to become his friends. After that Mr Popov's family forgave him and let him come back to his house, and all members of his family became members of the 'Unique Side Show Ring'.

Although Baby Samuel had until now not noticed much that was going on in VillageAll, when Mr Smith and his friends in First End told him about the 'Unique Side Show Ring' he began to take more interest in the affairs of VillageAll and wanted to know more.

At the same time, Baby Samuel was again finding it difficult to buy enough bread and vegetables from First End shops. Well, Baby Samuel, who was still growing bigger, was now almost four times as big as anybody and everybody in VillageAll, and he needed lots and lots of bread and vegetables to keep his hunger away. But the shops in First End didn't have enough; they were already selling all that the First Field could produce, and it was not enough.

One day Baby Samuel said he would farm new land in First Field to make more corn and more vegetables. Baby Samuel started immediately and, because he was so big and so powerful, in no time he was farming the new land, which doubled the size of First Field, and its products. Because Baby Samuel could work so quickly and so easily, he could produce the corn and the vegetables much more quickly than the other farmers, who would stand bewildered and stare at him in amazement as he darted around in a flash, with huge ploughs and other equipment that would take a whole lot of people many days to move.

Baby Samuel now could again buy enough bread and vegetables from the First End bakery and First End grocer, who were very happy because, thanks to Baby Samuel, their businesses increased.

While Baby Samuel was getting more interested in VillageAll affairs and its supply of food, Mr Smith was getting more worried about keeping in touch with his friends in all parts of VillageAll. Mr Smith liked to visit his friends but he was getting busier and his friends now lived in places in all parts of VillageAll so he could no longer visit them all as much as he wanted.

So Mr Smith wanted to keep in touch with his friends without going to visit them. This occupied Mr Smith's thoughts for a long time, and finally he had an idea.

Mr Smith announced to his friends in First End that he would start the 'Busy Bee Circle'. Mr Smith explained that he was going to put up a 'Busy Bee Circle'[58] notice board on the front of his smith shop, and invite his friends in all parts of VillageAll to send messengers to his shop and put up a memo on the notice board with information and news about themselves. That way anybody who looks over the 'Busy Bee Circle' notice board could find information about what was happening to their friends and everybody else, and what was happening in other parts of VillageAll.

Everybody in First End thought it was a very good idea. Well, almost everybody, because Mr Pompidou thought it was a silly idea and said, "Who would want to hear other people's news anyway?" Messrs Schmidt and Cortez said that if Mr Smith wanted to know their news he should send his messenger to them instead.

Mr Smith visited as many of his friends in Middle End and Far End as he could to explain about his idea and to invite them to join the 'Busy Bee Circle'. Many of Mr Smith's friends accepted his invitation and started to send messengers every day with notices of their news. The messengers would of course return with as much news and information from the board as they could remember. Soon Mr Smith's friends in First End could see that the information that Mr Smith obtained from the

'Busy Bee Circle' was very useful for his business and for making new friends and keeping old friends. Before long, most of Mr Smith's friends in First End, including Mr Schmidt and Mr Cortez, joined the 'Busy Bee Circle' and found the exchange of information and news as useful as Mr Smith had found earlier. Even Mr Pompidou eventually joined, even though what he really wanted was to have his own 'circle' for information.

Soon after the 'Busy Bee Circle' became part of the life of VillageAll, the mysterious illness which had once before come to First End, returned, and was even worse this time[59]. Everybody in First End was ill. Not only First End, because in New End Baby Samuel was especially ill, which was bad news to both First End and New End, because only Baby Samuel could farm the new big cornfield in First Field and only Baby Samuel could bring so much fish and game to the shops of First End. People in First End said that 'Friday was black' because Baby Samuel always caught a lot of fish in the big river on Fridays, and now not only was there no bread in the shops, but there was also no fish on Friday.

Although, as before, some people heard that somebody found medicine for the mysterious illness, nobody actually saw the medicine, and nobody was cured by any medicine.

But many people in First End talked about the Knabers again and how they brought the mysterious illness, and some people said they saw strange-looking little men entering Baby Samuel's house at night. Other people said they saw Knabers carrying food and medicine to Baby Samuel's house and also to the Smiths'. Soon everybody in First End started to feel better about the Knabers because they believed that they would cure Baby Samuel and he would be back working in the farms and bringing the food.

Well, almost everybody, because Mrs Pompidou said to her husband, "If the Knabers didn't bring the illness first, we would not need them to cure us now." Mr Pompidou said that he could not agree more.

Although everybody in First End was struck by the mysterious illness, some people were more struck than others. Mr & Mrs Schmidt were struck with the illness very badly and their neighbours were very worried because sometimes Mr Schmidt was behaving very strangely. And that was bad news for Mr Moschel.

Mr Moschel was an old friend of the Smiths. He was very poor and although he had been living in First End for a long time, he never had his own house and always lived with relatives and friends. Mr Moschel was always moving houses because people said they didn't like him as a neighbour because he always borrowed food and never gave any back. Although this was not true, many people in First End believed it was, and were not friendly to Mr Moschel, especially the Schmidts. The Schmidts were very unfriendly to Mr Moschel, even when they were fit and healthy. But when they were ill they were even less friendly and when Mr Schmidt was very ill and behaving strangely, he was most unkind to Mr Moschel[60]. So Mr Moschel asked Mr Smith to help him. Mr Moschel said that although he liked living in

First End, he long ago lived in Middle End and would very much like to have his own place and live there again. Well, Mr Smith at that time was also struck with the mysterious illness, but was not very ill and was not behaving strangely, so Mr Smith promised Mr Moschel that he would find a new home for him in Middle End as soon as he got better[61].

Because of the 'Busy Bee Circle', people in Middle End and Far End heard about the illness in First End and New End, and stayed home instead of visiting friends.

Mr Watanabe wanted to walk to First End to visit his ill friends, but Mrs Watanabe said he had better not because although Baby Samuel was now friendly with the Watanabes, she had heard that when giant babies became ill they became much less friendly. Well, Mr Watanabe now listened much more carefully to what Mrs Watanabe said and so he agreed instead to take a walk, together with Mrs Watanabe, around their garden-in-house.

When Mr & Mrs Watanabe reached the back of the house they saw that the fruit tree in the Chens' garden was laden with fruit and was leaning over their wall so most of the fruit was hanging over the Watanabes' garden. Mr Watanabe said to his wife, "Well, that decides it. This tree belongs in our garden."

He immediately set about to rebuild the wall to bring the tree, and a bit of the Chens' garden inside the Watanabes' garden[62]. By the time the Chens realised what was happening, the tree, and a bit of their garden, were already inside the Watanabes' garden. Mr Chen was not a big man, and although he had many children they were all much smaller than him, and much, much smaller than Mr Watanabe. And, because of the mysterious illness, Mr Chen could not call on his friends in First End for help. Mrs Chen was very unhappy and said she was never again going to be friends with the Watanabes.

CHAPTER XV

The mysterious illness continued to make the people of First End and Baby Samuel in New End miserable because nobody knew how to cure it. So the men of First End decided to restart their 'Men's Club' because they wanted to do things that made them forget about the illness. Although Baby Samuel was still just a baby, he now walked taller than all the houses and all the trees of VillageAll. Baby Samuel was not only invited but was asked if he agreed to the idea of the 'Men's Club' restarting. Well, Baby Samuel said that if Mr Smith agreed then he would also agree, so the club was restarted.

The men of First End started to meet again every day in their club to do the things men liked to do and to try to forget about the mysterious illness. And everybody started gambling. Well, almost everybody, because some men said that gambling was not a good idea, and 'look what happened the last time'.

At first the bets were small because the men did remember 'what happened the last time', but they found that making small bets didn't make them forget about the mysterious illness.

So the more the men felt ill the bigger they wanted to bet. Especially Mr Schmidt, who was very, very ill. Mr Schmidt kept increasing his bets and so everybody else also increased their bets, and some of the men were frightened to see how ill Mr Schmidt was, and didn't want to bet with him, or against him. As the bets were getting higher and higher, the men agreed that they should make 'special betting nights', only once a week.

The first of these special betting nights went well as Mr Schmidt was feeling better and didn't make very big bets. But on the second special betting night, not only Mr Schmidt, but also Mr Watanabe, Mr Luigi and Baby Samuel all said they felt very ill and started to make big bets. Of course, Baby Samuel could not sit in the same room with the other men, so Mr Smith and Mr Pompidou were making his bets for him.

Well, that night the stakes were high, as they had never been before, and that night the men stayed up terribly late, and made terribly big bets, mostly terribly big bad bets[63].

And the men should have remembered, because of what happened the last time, that when you make terribly big bets, you lose terribly big.

Although everybody lost that night, Mr Schmidt and Mr Watanabe lost the most.

And although the mysterious illness soon disappeared, everybody in First End had a miserable time being healthy, poor and hungry, and many people said that it was like curing an illness that you don't know anything about, with a non-curable disease that you know everything about!

The Schmidts had to move to a much smaller house, with almost no garden, and Mr Schmidt lost much weight and became very quiet and said he would never again enter the 'Men's Club'. But for Mr Watanabe it was a disaster. Mr Watanabe had lost all his bets and could not pay back what he owed. And especially, Mr Watanabe could not pay back what he owed to Baby Samuel. Mr Watanabe had said that Baby Samuel didn't know how to bet because he was just a baby, after all, so he said it would be easy to out bet him, and he made very big bets against him.

Well, although Baby Samuel was just a baby, and babies don't worry about what people say about them, Mr Smith was not a baby and Mr Smith worried indeed about what people said about Baby Samuel, and when Mr Smith was upset, so was Baby Samuel.

And so both Mr Smith and Baby Samuel were already very upset with Mr Watanabe. And now when Baby Samuel tried to collect his dues, and Mr Watanabe said he had nothing left, well, Baby Samuel suddenly had a bad headache, like the headache he always had when he heard babies crying. And when Baby Samuel had a baby-crying kind of headache it was bad news indeed. For everybody. But especially for Mr Watanabe. Baby Samuel clutched his head in his two big hands and ran along The StreetAll to Far End. In a few hops he was standing in front of the Watanabes' house. Baby Samuel's big fists, which were now considerably bigger than when they had come across the Watanabes' wall with no door, rose up in the air, and came down on the wall surrounding the Watanabes' house, and this time brought the whole wall down, every bit of it, right round the house.

Baby Samuel stood there admiring his achievement, the second Watanabe wall achievement, and his headache was already getting better. He then stepped into the Watanabes' garden-in-house which was now mostly a garden with little house, and found a nice shady corner by the pond and there sat down and wiped his brow.

Mrs Watanabe, sitting in the house, who didn't hear any preludes this time, and who was not easily frightened, nor given to hysterics, nearly fainted when the wall all around her crumpled, and she saw the hulk of Baby Samuel towering over her house and garden. Mrs Watanabe suddenly felt as if she was sitting in the street and waved her arms at Baby Samuel, as if to shoo him away, but nearly fainted again when, instead, she saw Baby Samuel wandering into the garden.

Well, although Baby Samuel was just a baby, he was a giant baby, and giant babies like to do things their own way, and everybody had to like their way.

Baby Samuel told the Watanabes that they were not going to have a wall around their house, ever again, and that he was going to come to their garden and sit in his favourite spot whenever he liked. And as for Mr Watanabe, well, that was not the end of his troubles.

Because Mrs Watanabe was very, very angry with Mr Watanabe and told him he was never going out again, and that he was to always make Baby Samuel happy and look after him whenever he came to their garden.

With the Watanabe wall gone, Mrs Chen was quick to get her husband to rebuild *their* wall so that they had their full garden again, and with it their famous fruit tree. But although Mrs Chen was now happier, she told her husband not to speak to the Watanabes over *their* new wall because … "Mr Watanabe should not have gone to the 'Men's Club' to make bad bets," she said.

Although Mr Smith was not one of the big losers on that terrible night, he didn't feel very well afterwards, and Mrs Smith told him he was to have some rest. Mr Smith started to spend less time in his smith shop and started to ask Baby Samuel to help him with many things, which of course Baby Samuel was happy to do. Mr Pompidou also didn't lose much, and, like Mr Smith, didn't feel very well, but Mrs Pompidou, unlike Mrs Smith, pushed Mr Pompidou out of the house to go and find new friends and get better.

The only winners of the 'Men's Club's terrible night were Baby Samuel and Mr Popov. Both Baby Samuel and Mr Popov won their bets *and* felt fit and strong afterwards.

So, after the terrible night, Mr Popov in First End, and Baby Samuel in New End became the most important people in VillageAll.

Mr Popov told his friends in the 'Unique Side Show Ring' that he was now much fitter than before and that Baby Samuel would soon be ill again. Although Mr Popov's friends didn't see any signs of Baby Samuel getting ill again, they liked Mr Popov and told him he was their best friend and Baby Samuel was not their friend, whether he was ill or not.

Everybody in VillageAll agreed that Mr Popov was now fitter and stronger and more important. Well, almost everybody, because Mr Smith, who was not feeling very well, said that Mr Popov's 'Unique Side Show Ring' was as bad as First End's 'Men's Club' and as good at making people healthier and fitter.

CHAPTER XVI

Baby Samuel was barely eighteen-months-old, but was already five times as big as anybody and everybody in VillageAll, and was still growing. Baby Samuel was sure to be even bigger by the time he celebrated his second birthday.

As Baby Samuel continued to grow bigger, his house continued to grow smaller for him. So Baby Samuel was soon rebuilding big parts of his house, raising the roofs and making doors and windows larger. He made the house much bigger than it needed to be this time because Baby Samuel didn't want to rebuild his house again soon. Although Baby Samuel knew the people of VillageAll and had many friends, he was so much bigger than everybody that when he looked way down at the people scurrying around him he could not help feeling they were so *different*, as if they were not people at all. Of course, Baby Samuel was just a baby, and babies don't think of *themselves* as different, so it must be everybody else who were different.

A growing giant baby had a growing giant appetite, and Baby Samuel was again running out of food because First End shops didn't have enough bacon, or enough beef, or enough chicken, or enough cheese to sell him. First End shopkeepers said to Baby Samuel that there were not enough pigs or cows, or chickens in all of First End to feed him and all the people of First End. Because, of course, as Baby Samuel was getting bigger, so was First End, and many more people now lived there than before.

Baby Samuel, who already had a big corn field and a big vegetable farm in First Field, this time decided to start new animal farms in his own land across the river, which he had anyway decided was part of New End.

With his giant energy and giant power, Baby Samuel soon set up a pig farm, a cattle ranch, a chicken farm and a dairy farm in New End, and started to bring their products to the shops and food factories, not only in First End but in all of VillageAll. That way Baby Samuel could always buy enough food to keep the hunger away. The shops and food factories in VillageAll grew much bigger and made very good business because they had good supplies and many customers.

Around that time Mr Smith started to feel better and decided he would help his friend Mr Moschel to get a new home, as he had promised.

One day, Mr Smith took Mr Moschel to the Mustaphas' house in Middle End. Although Mr Mustapha was not home at that time, Mr Smith told Mrs Mustapha that Mr Moschel was going to live with them, and that the Mustaphas had to give Mr Moschel one of the rooms to become his new home[64]. Although Mrs

Mustapha, unlike people in First End, didn't feel unkind towards Mr Moschel, she was very angry because the Mustaphas' house was small and they had a lot of children. But what could Mrs Mustapha do? Mr Smith was such an important person in VillageAll, and had a baby who was bigger than all of the Mustaphas' small house.

Mr Moschel has lived in the Mustaphas' house ever since, but Mr Moschel has yet to find the kind neighbours he left First End for!

Around the time that Mr Moschel started to live in the Mustaphas' house, Baby Samuel told Mr Smith about the big beehives[65] he had found on the other side of the river. Mr Smith, who liked honey, was very excited and said he would teach Baby Samuel how to take the honey out of the beehives. Mr Smith also told Baby Samuel that he wanted beehives in VillageAll on this side of the river, and said that it might be a good idea to take some to Mr Mustapha in Middle End, because he was a good grocer. Well, Baby Samuel was now also excited, not only because of the honey, but also because his friends in First End and in Middle End would think he was clever.

So the next day Baby Samuel brought back with him from New End a big beehive and he and Mr Smith went to see Mr Mustapha. Mr Mustapha was still upset with Mr Smith because of Mr Moschel, but he liked getting beehives from Baby Samuel and said many people in Middle End, and also in First End and Far End want to have honey. In a few days, Baby Samuel appeared at Mr

Mustapha's shop with a huge sack which had many beehives.

This was big news in VillageAll and everybody in First End said how clever Mr Smith and Baby Samuel were. Well, almost everybody, because Mr Pompidou said to his wife that some of the beehives did not look like beehives at all and there would be no honey coming out of them, and who knows what else one day would come out of them.

Well, the honey business made Mr Mustapha more important in VillageAll and many more customers than before came to his grocer's shop. But not only customers: many people from First End and also from Far End came to visit Mr Mustapha to see the beehives. Mr Mustapha was very happy to have more *customers*, but he was not at all happy to have *visitors*. Mrs Mustapha complained to her husband because visitors, especially from First End, came at all times and came into the Mustaphas' house and into their garden without being invited, and said, "Visitors only bring trouble with them." Mr Mustapha said he couldn't agree more and said that visitors took his time so he could not run his business well as he had always done before.

Meanwhile, Mr Popov was getting more friends to join his 'Unique Side Show Ring', which was getting bigger and more famous in VillageAll. The Chens were the last to become members, and that pleased Mr Popov because Mr & Mrs Chen had a big family and a big house and many friends. Mr & Mrs Phong were among these friends, and were very good friends of the Chens.

So the Phongs were very happy to join the 'ring' when the Chens asked them to do so. But the Phongs were also friends of the Pompidous, and Mr Pompidou often visited them and had tea with them.

After the Phongs joined the 'Unique Side Show Ring' Mr Phong told Mr Pompidou he didn't have any more tea to offer him, and didn't want his visits anymore.

Well, Mr Pompidou was very angry indeed. Mr Pompidou was especially angry because he knew that it was Mr Popov's 'Unique Side Show Ring', which was the cause of the trouble with the Phongs, and was worried that the 'ring' was getting bigger and more famous in VillageAll.

Mr Pompidou talked to his friends in First End but nobody had any good ideas. Then he talked to Baby Samuel who did have a good idea: Baby Samuel suggested he would fetch some interesting, and different herbs from New End far across the river, which Mr Pompidou would offer the Phongs this time instead of drinking their tea, to try to keep them as his friends and then persuade them to leave the 'ring'.

Mr Pompidou thought it was an excellent idea, so Baby Samuel set off straight away to look for the herbs. Although Baby Samuel can sometimes have very good ideas, and although he wanted to help Mr Pompidou, he was really just a baby, and babies can easily mistake herbs with weeds and other interesting plants. But Baby Samuel did make a big effort and brought back a bundle of what he said were tasty herbs from New End.

Mr Pompidou took the bundle of herbs and went to visit the Phongs[66]. At first Mr Phong didn't let Mr Pompidou in, but when Mr Pompidou offered him the bundle of herbs he reluctantly let him in and asked his wife to prepare a herbal drink, using Mr Pompidou's offering. Mrs Phong soon brought a tray with drinks for the three of them. Although Mr Pompidou was the guest, he humoured Mr Phong by insisting that he took the first sip. Mr Phong was not very keen on trying Mr Pompidou's herbal drink, but he accepted the invitation and took a mouthful of the tea. Mr Pompidou was looking at Mr Phong with a somewhat hesitant smile, when he saw Mr Phong's face getting red, his eyes narrowing and his cheeks puffing out, before all the tea that Mr Phong drank exploded out of his face in a shower that drenched all around him, leaving poor Mr Phong in a fit of coughs and splutters.

Well, the herbs that Baby Samuel collected might have been good for something, although nobody was ever going to find out. What was sure, as poor Mr Phong found out, was what those herbs were *not* good for. As Mr Phong said, horse manure would have made better tea; at least it would not have burnt through his tongue *and* his cheeks!

Mr Pompidou didn't try to visit the Phongs anymore, but Baby Samuel said he would continue to look for more interesting herbs because, you never know, he might want to visit the Phongs himself sometime.

Mr Pompidou, it seemed, was not doing well keeping friends in Far End and Middle End. But Mrs Pompidou was still pushing him to go out and make friends and become important again, so Mr Pompidou started to see his friends in First End more often. Especially, Mr Pompidou started to see Mr Schmidt more often. Mr Schmidt had now recovered his health and he also wanted to make friends and wanted to become important again. Mr Pompidou and Mr Schmidt were now meeting quite often and became more and more friendly with each other. Mr Luigi who had suffered a lot after the events of the 'terrible night' had also recovered well and wanted to make friends and forget about the past. Mr Luigi was happy when he realised that Mr Pompidou and Mr Schmidt had the same idea, and the three became very friendly.

Although Mr Pompidou, Mr Schmidt and Mr Luigi were now healthy and friendly, they were not yet important in VillageAll, as once they were before.

So, one day the three families announced that they were going to live together in one house[67]. New House would be very big, much bigger than any other house in all of VillageAll, except for Baby Samuel's house, and quite a bit bigger than the Smiths'.

The three families said that New House would get bigger later as more of their neighbours moved to live in it.

Well, that was big news indeed and soon New House became very famous in VillageAll, and the three families became much more important than before. Baby Samuel, who was now taking more interest in what was going on in VillageAll, said New House was OK because his friends lived in it and because it was still much smaller than his house. Well, Baby Samuel was just a baby, and babies liked to have friends close by, and giant babies wanted to have the biggest toys!

CHAPTER XVII

Although the Smiths and Pompidous were not very good friends a lot of the time, especially Mrs Pompidou and Mrs Smith, they had lived next door to each other such a long time, and sometimes it was useful for Mr Smith and Mr Pompidou to talk and do things together. One thing Mr Smith and Mr Pompidou sometimes did together was to take a walk to Middle End to do their shopping at Mr Mustapha's butcher shop. Mr Mustapha was the biggest butcher in Middle End, and although there were butchers in First End also, Mr Mustapha's shop sometimes had the best chicken meat and the lowest prices.

One day Mr Smith heard, through the 'Busy Bee Circle', that Mr Mustapha was not going to sell any more meat to people in First End, and especially not to Mr Smith, because Mrs Mustapha was upset about Mr Smith making Mr Moschel live in their house. Well, Mr Smith was quite angry about this news, and when he told his next door neighbour, Mr Pompidou was also angry. So Mr Smith and Mr Pompidou set off immediately to visit the Mustaphas[68].

Mr Pompidou and Mr Smith went to the Mustaphas' house first, because they wanted to get Mr Moschel to help them. Mr Mustapha was not home when they arrived, and when Mrs Mustapha opened the door and saw Mr Smith's face she let out such a scream that the walls of the house started to shake and rattle, and continued to shake and rattle as Mrs Mustapha kept up the loudest scream anybody had ever heard.

Now, Mr Mustapha's shop was quite near the house, and it so happened that the chickens that Mr Mustapha sold in his shop came from Baby Samuel's chicken farm, and it so happened that at the very moment that Mrs Mustapha started to scream, Baby Samuel had just arrived at Mr Mustapha's shop with a new load of chickens.

Mr Mustapha had told his wife that if Mr Moschel gave her any trouble she should scream loud enough for him to hear her in his shop. So when Mrs Mustapha's very loud scream screeched into the shop, Mr Mustapha answered with a loud yell of his own and leapt from behind the counter of his shop heading to the door.

Baby Samuel, who had walked across the enormous lands of New End and across the big river, with a very big load of chickens, was looking forward to Mr Mustapha greeting him warmly, as he always did, and offering him a nice big cold drink and a friendly chat, as he always did, before they got down to business. Mrs Mustapha's scream pierced Baby Samuel's ears just as he was setting down the chicken load. It was a 'baby cry' kind of scream, the worst kind if you were Baby Samuel, because it was the kind of scream that gave him that terrible headache. Mr Mustapha's quite sharp yell, which followed immediately, made his headache much worse. Baby Samuel, with his head throbbing from the continued screaming, and his mind bothered, leaned down and tried to look into the shop. It was at that moment that Mr Mustapha shot out of the shop's door and smashed into Baby Samuel's big face. Mr Mustapha quickly recovered himself, but Baby Samuel didn't. His face was now hurting as well as his head, and he didn't hear or understand one word as Mr Mustapha, with arms flailing, explained about Mr Moschel living with them and about his wife being in danger and about him asking her to scream, and … and …

Although Baby Samuel didn't *understand* what was happening, he *knew* that something bad was happening because it made him feel so bad. Well, he was just a baby, after all, and babies don't understand things, they just feel good or feel bad. So, when Mr Mustapha finally finished his explanations and ran to his house, Baby Samuel got up and, clutching his head, followed Mr Mustapha.

When Baby Samuel's bleary eyes made out the scene in front of him, with Mrs Mustapha, still screaming, facing Mr Smith, Mr Pompidou and Mr Moschel, Baby Samuel knew exactly what was bad, and he shouted at the three men. Well, even if Baby Samuel didn't intend to frighten everybody, a giant's shouting didn't only sound like thunder, it also *felt* like thunder, and even though the three men didn't know what Baby Samuel was saying, they understood quite well what he was telling them, and all three quickly left, each going his own way. That finally stopped Mrs Mustapha's screaming, and that finally stopped Baby Samuel's headache, and that finally let Mr Mustapha be warm and friendly and bring Baby Samuel a big cool drink, as he had always done.

Although Mr Moschel had gone away, he had not gone far, and was just round the corner from the Mustaphas' house and stood in the shade of a large tree watching as Mr Mustapha and Baby Samuel chatted like old friends. That made Mr Moschel feel bad because *he* never had friends even when he very much wanted to have friends. But Mr Moschel was clever, and he could see how in VillageAll nobody wanted to do anything which might upset Baby Samuel, and so decided that from now on he was going to try very hard to become Baby Samuel's best friend.

Mr Mustapha immediately sent his messenger to the 'Busy Bee Circle' board to tell everybody in VillageAll how Baby Samuel got angry with Mr Smith and Mr Pompidou and shouted at them and made them run away from the Mustaphas' house.

It was very big news indeed.

Because although everybody knew that Mr Smith and Mr Pompidou were much smaller than Baby Samuel, nobody thought that Baby Samuel would get angry with them. And if Baby Samuel was friends with Mr Smith and Mr Pompidou and never got angry with them, well, they could still be very important people in VillageAll. But if Baby Samuel got angry with Mr Smith and Mr

Pompidou, how could they be very important people in VillageAll?

Well, it was such shocking news.

Especially for Mr Smith.

Because until now the Smiths, although they no longer lived in the biggest house in VillageAll, well, nobody could live in a house bigger than Baby Samuel's, they still had the biggest garden in all of VillageAll. But if Mr Smith was no longer one of the most important persons in VillageAll, how could the Smiths keep the biggest garden, or the big house? And if Baby Samuel got angry with Mr Smith and Mr Pompidou, well, it meant Baby Samuel could get angry with anybody, and everybody, in VillageAll!

And so on that day the people of VillageAll thought that Baby Samuel was not only the biggest and strongest person in VillageAll, he was now also the most important person.

It was the first time ever that the most important person in VillageAll was a baby.

Everybody in VillageAll was happy because Baby Samuel was such a nice baby and was making the shops of VillageAll bigger.

Well, almost everybody, because some people, like Mr Popov and Mr Chen and their 'Unique Side Show Ring', didn't like Baby Samuel and didn't want him to be the most important person in VillageAll, and said it was not good that a giant baby got angry with anybody.

And although Mr Smith was no longer one of the most important persons in VillageAll, he was, after all, Baby Samuel's father and so was happy that Baby Samuel was now the most important person in VillageAll, even if it meant that the Smiths had a smaller house and a much smaller garden.

Baby Samuel was now so big and so important that, although he was just a baby, many people, especially in Middle End and Far End started to forget that he was just a baby, and started to think of him as just big, powerful, and sometimes angry.

And although Baby Samuel was a giant, and giants frighten children, the children of VillageAll were not frightened of Baby Samuel, because they knew he was just a baby, and because their parents always told them he was such a good baby even if he was a giant. And the children of VillageAll wanted to grow big like Baby Samuel, and do the daring things only he could do. Especially, the children of VillageAll dreamed about crossing the big river, and going to explore the New End lands that lay beyond, just like Baby Samuel did.

But most of all, the children of VillageAll, especially the children of poor families, wanted to be able to eat big meals like Baby Samuel.

Although Baby Samuel was eating big meals, he was ever hungrier because he was not only a giant but was still getting bigger. Baby Samuel wanted to grow more food in his new farms in New End. And although Baby Samuel was so big and strong and fast, he could not work all his farms in New End by himself. But although people could easily work in First, Middle and Far Fields, no one could work in New Field in New End, because nobody in VillageAll could cross the river; only Baby Samuel could.

So Baby Samuel had an idea: he would carry people across the river so they could work on his farms.

When people in VillageAll heard of Baby Samuel's idea they were astonished and very worried because, until Baby Samuel did, nobody had ever crossed the big river. But Baby Samuel was a giant, even if he was just a baby, and the people of VillageAll didn't think they could do what giants could do. Especially the older people of VillageAll, they were frightened of big rivers and of faraway lands that nobody knew about.

Mr Pompidou said to his wife, "What if people fell in the river?"

Mrs Pompidou said she could not agree more, and added, "And what if there were strange creatures in New End?"

But the Pompidou children thought the idea of crossing the big river on Baby Samuel's back and going to New End was the most exciting idea they had ever heard! And not only the Pompidou children: most of the children and young people of VillageAll started to get excited about the idea, especially the Smiths' children who were so excited when they heard Mrs Smith telling her husband how clever Baby Samuel was to think of this idea, and how exciting it must be to explore New End just like Baby Samuel did every day.

CHAPTER XVIII

Although Baby Samuel didn't understand what Mr Popov's 'Unique Side Show Ring' was all about, he hated it and said that all the people who joined it were bad people. Well, he was just a baby, and babies want everybody to like them, and they hate people who don't like them. And because Baby Samuel hated the 'Unique Side Show Ring', all his friends in First End also hated it and told him that they were worried because it was getting bigger and stronger.

Baby Samuel didn't want the 'Unique Side Show Ring' to get bigger, and remembered about the Phongs' quarrel with Mr Pompidou when Mr Phong joined the 'ring'. Although the Phongs had a small house and no garden, they lived next door to the Chens and were good friends with them, and Mr Phong had a small grocery shop in Far End, where the Chens did their shopping. Mr Phong's shop was one of the few shops in Far End where Baby Samuel had not yet done any shopping, so he thought that if he could do business with Mr Phong's shop he would have a better supply for his food, and he would become Mr Phong's friend, and then he would also become Mr Chen's friend[69].

Although Baby Samuel also remembered about the 'herb tea incident', which Mr Phong had with Mr Pompidou, he still thought it was a good idea to get some interesting herbs from New End to offer Mr Phong as a gift when he visited his shop to sell him vegetables. But this time, Baby Samuel thought, he was going to be extra careful about the herbs!

So Baby Samuel went across the river and to the farthest corner of New End, and spent a lot of time and took a lot of care picking good herbs. He then checked the herbs with his friends in First End, and when he was sure they were good herbs he took a load of vegetables from his farm in First Field and went to Mr Phong's shop in Far End.

Mr Phong was not expecting a visit from Baby Samuel. Mr Phong had been told by Mr Chen and Mr Popov that Baby Samuel was bad. So when Mr Phong saw the hulk of Baby Samuel approaching his shop he was both terrified and angry. Mr Phong didn't see the babyish smile on Baby Samuel's face as he offered the bundle of herbs because Mr Phong at that moment neither wanted, nor dared, raise his head way up to look at Baby Samuel's face. But when Mr Phong heard the word 'herbs' he exploded with a shriek that rang out throughout the neighbourhood. The whole Chen family came out, with Mr Popov, who happened to be visiting them at that time. Mrs Phong, Mrs Aung and the Khemeras and other families also came out. And all were yelling and screaming and shaking their fists at Baby Samuel. It was a racket, the kind of noise that gave Baby

Samuel that terrible headache and made him do strange things even when he didn't mean to. Mr Phong, feeling stronger now with the people around him, grabbed a garden rake and lunged at Baby Samuel's legs, hitting them repeatedly with the rack. As he felt the pain in his legs, Baby Samuel now not only had the terrible headache but was also very angry, and, with one shake of one leg, he flung Mr Phong way up in the air and then crushed his shop with his big foot. Mr Phong, who had landed in the backyard of his shop nearly died from the shock, from his very painful landing, and from the rubble of his shop that landed on top of him.

The racket stopped immediately as everybody looked at the crushed shop and at Mr Phong's body under the rubble. Well, almost everybody, because Mrs Phong looked up at Baby Samuel's face with a piercing look that carried a message, a message that Baby Samuel neither could, nor wanted to understand.

CHAPTER XIX

After Baby Samuel smashed Mr Phong's shop, all the people in VillageAll said he was a bad baby. Well, almost all, because some people said that Mr Phong was bad and he should not have joined Mr Popov's 'Unique Side Show Ring'. Although Mr Phong was their friend, Mr Popov and Mr Chen were pleased because after that incident many people wanted to join the 'ring' to explain to everybody how bad Baby Samuel was.

Then one day rain completely stopped falling on First Field.

Well, almost completely, because there were days when rain still fell, but it was so little that all the farmers of First Field became worried because they realised that their crops were going to be very poor that season.

Although enough rain was still falling on Middle Field, Far Field and New Field, it was *their* rain, which would not reach First Field or help to water its crops.

So, that season, although the crops of Middle Field, Far Field and New Field were good and healthy, First Field's crops were too few, too little, and too dried out to feed the people of First End.

Baby Samuel was still buying all his bread and vegetables from First End shops, and although he was one of the farmers of First Field and knew how bad the crops were, he only became upset when he tried to buy some bread but found that the shop had none. Well, he was just a baby and babies don't get upset about crops, but they do get upset when they go hungry!

Although other people in First End were also hungry, Baby Samuel's giant appetite was much bigger than anybody else's so he was much more hungry than anybody else.

And although people in First End knew that rain was still falling in the other fields, they didn't see that they could change the way things had been for hundreds of years.

But Baby Samuel was just a baby, a hungry baby, a giant hungry baby.

And Baby Samuel had an idea.

So Baby Samuel talked to Mr Smith and Mr Pompidou and Mr Schmidt, and to other friends in First End to explain his idea. Baby Samuel also talked to his friends in Middle End and Far End, especially Mr Watanabe, who was still kept at home by Mrs Watanabe.

And everybody agreed with Baby Samuel's idea.

Well, almost everybody, because some of his friends thought that Baby Samuel's idea was a bad idea.

But nobody said so to Baby Samuel.

Everybody said how good his idea was.

Because even though Baby Samuel's friends didn't think he was a bad baby, they knew what he could do when he had a bad headache, and they didn't want to give him one, ever.

Baby Samuel got to work immediately.

Baby Samuel was so big, so powerful, and could work so fast that people in all three ends of VillageAll could see him simultaneously as he rushed from one field to another, with sheets of metal, ducts, timber and other material and equipment.

Soon people could see the new construction taking shape: Baby Samuel was building an aqueduct system across the ravines that separated the three fields. The ravines were so deep and so wide that only a giant could build across them. VillageAll people stood in amazement and awe as they watched the construction taking place at such enormous speed.

In no time at all, the ducts were in place and water started to pour into the stricken First Field to revive its ravished crops.

From that time on, water would flow across all three fields, and the rain that fell on one field would run across to water the crops of the other two fields.

Everybody in First End was saying how great Baby Samuel's idea was. And although people in Middle End and Far End didn't mind sharing their rain with First End *this* year, they did wonder if they would get their share of the rain when the drought was at their end of VillageAll, or when there just was not enough rain for all three fields.

Some people in VillageAll also said that Baby Samuel was in such a hurry that he didn't construct the aqueduct properly. They pointed at the precious water leaking from the ducts and the wobbling ravine structures and other 'babyish' parts of the construction. But, as Mrs Smith said, people had better be happy because Baby Samuel did something nobody else could do and, well if the ducts break down then Baby Samuel would always be there to fix them, wouldn't he?

Baby Samuel was happy with his work, not only because First End shops would once again have plenty of food, but because, with rain 'shared' all over VillageAll, he could now buy his bread and vegetables in shops all over VillageAll, so he would not be hungry again.

Mr Watanabe had been very happy to hear about Baby Samuel's idea for sharing the rain across VillageAll because Mr Watanabe had his own idea of 'sharing'.

Although Mr Watanabe had been kept home by Mrs Watanabe, he had been very busy. Mr Watanabe had built a large, brand new smith shop in his back garden. He filled it with new and clever machines for making new and clever implements.

Mr Watanabe talked to Baby Samuel about 'sharing' his new smith shop with the rest of VillageAll. Mr Watanabe was still under strict instruction from Mrs

Watanabe to always keep Baby Samuel happy, so he wanted to make sure Baby Samuel didn't dislike his idea.

Baby Samuel thought it was a good idea and asked Mrs Watanabe to let Mr Watanabe out so he could go to all parts of VillageAll to offer his new and clever products.

Mr Watanabe was soon travelling everywhere, and everywhere finding good customers for his products.

Although Mr Smith was still an important person in VillageAll and still had many friends, his smith shop had become old, with old equipment making old implements, and Mr Smith said to Mrs Smith that, frankly speaking, he preferred to do gardening and weeding instead. Even in First End, Mr Schmidt now had a bigger smith shop than Mr Smith's.

But Mr Watanabe's smith shop was the biggest in the whole of VillageAll, and soon became the best and most famous.

CHAPTER XX

Baby Samuel was now rapidly approaching his second birthday.

And although Baby Samuel had kept growing bigger and was now six times as big as anybody and everybody in VillageAll, he had grown only a little bigger in the last few months, and he felt that maybe he would not grow bigger after he became two years old.

Which would be just as well.

Because even without growing any bigger, it was already not easy for Baby Samuel to talk with, or visit, or do business with people, who would have to crane their heads high up if they wanted to look at Baby Samuel's face, instead of his knees. It was as if they had to find the top of the tallest tree every time they talked to Baby Samuel.

Baby Samuel's house was now neither too big nor too small, and he just needed to enlarge a couple of back rooms and the kitchen to make himself more comfortable.

Baby Samuel announced he was going to have a big birthday party, and invited his friends from First End,

Middle End and Far End. And although Baby Samuel didn't especially like the Chens, he invited Mr & Mrs Chen and *all* their children, because Mr Smith and Mr Pompidou told Baby Samuel that he had an enormous house, and if he couldn't invite the Chens with all their children, then who could?

Baby Samuel also invited some people who were not his friends because Mr Smith told Baby Samuel, "You are not really important until you are important with people you don't like."

Baby Samuel's second birthday party was the biggest party VillageAll had ever had. Baby Samuel's house was more spacious than the whole of First End, and there was enough food and soft drinks for more people than lived in the whole of VillageAll, and everybody enjoyed the food and drinks. Well, almost everybody, because Mrs Pompidou and Mrs Watanabe only ate the food they brought with them to the party. Mrs Pompidou had bad memories of the food at Baby Samuel's first birthday party, and thought that Mrs Smith helping Baby Samuel with the food this time could only make things worse! And although Mrs Watanabe didn't want to upset Baby Samuel, she was not used to going to parties and eating somebody else's food, especially not a giant baby's food, so she asked her husband to eat Baby Samuel's food and keep him happy.

Baby Samuel announced during the party that he was now going to be VillageAll's News Imp[70]. Baby Samuel said that the 'Busy Bee Circle' was too slow if you were in a hurry, and that he was going to be at the centre of a 'web' of news for VillageAll. He explained that he could move so quickly across VillageAll, so he was going to walk up and down VillageAll many times every day, and exchange news with anybody who wanted or had news, anywhere in the village. Baby Samuel said that even when he was working in his farms and going exploring in the big lands of New End, he would still convey the news more quickly than before because he could move so quickly compared to everybody else. Everybody in the party was excited about this news. Well, almost everybody, because Mrs Chen said, "What if Baby Samuel was really, really busy, and could not convey the news?"

Because Baby Samuel had listened to Mr Smith's advice, he had not only invited Mr & Mrs Chen, but also Mr & Mrs Popov and their friends. And even though Mr Popov was at Baby Samuel's party, and eating Baby Samuel's food and drinking his drinks, Mr Popov was trying to get members of his 'ring' to make one of their unique side shows to tell everybody that Baby Samuel was not really a very good baby.

One of the 'ring' members who was at the party was Mr Hofmann[71], who was Mr Schmidt's cousin. Mr Hofmann lived in a small house next to the Schmidts, and although Mr Hofmann liked Mr Schmidt, he was much younger than Mr Schmidt and was very good friends with Mr Popov, who was closer to him in age. So, Mr Popov was trying to talk Mr Hofmann into making a 'show', and didn't realise that Mr Schmidt was close by and could hear them. Suddenly, Mr Schmidt turned around and approached Mr Hofmann, and grabbing his arm he said, "You cannot do your 'show' at this party … don't listen to Mr Popov."

Mr Popov grabbed Mr Hofmann's other arm and said, "Don't listen to that toad Schmidt."

On hearing this, Mr Schmidt became very, very angry and his face turned purple red. He walked over to Mr Popov in a state of great agitation and challenged him to a fist fight, right there and then in front of all the party attendees. Now Mr Popov was the biggest man in VillageAll, strongly built and quite young, and Mr Schmidt was much smaller, thinner and older. So, although Mr Popov was very surprised, he was neither frightened nor worried about having a fist fight with Mr Schmidt, even though he might have preferred a different time and place, especially a time when he was not already enjoying himself, and a place where he and Mr Schmidt would not be under Baby Samuel's nose. But Mr Schmidt was quite serious and by now a group had gathered around the two and everybody was cheering and egging them on, and it was not long before Baby Samuel himself came over and, realising what the matter was, roared in a little laugh, that shook the walls and ceilings and caused all those near him to spill their drinks, and said that yes, they should fight outside in the yard, and that everybody should go out to watch[72].

So, that settled it. Mr Popov and Mr Schmidt stripped to their waists and Baby Samuel drew a circle in the ground. It was not a perfect circle; well, babies are not good at drawing circles, especially if they have to bend down four storeys to do it!

The fist fight didn't last very long. And it was not the strength or weakness of Mr Popov, nor the strength or weakness of Mr Schmidt that made it finish quickly. Although Baby Samuel was not fighting either Mr Popov or Mr Schmidt, he was there, and this was more important than anyone's strength.

When the fight started, Mr Schmidt, who was still very angry and very excited, rushed straight up to Mr Popov with a raised fist. Mr Popov, who was not as angry, nor as excited as Mr Schmidt had his fists up to start the fight, and he was strong enough to stop the coming blow from Mr Schmidt, if, that is, Baby Samuel didn't at that instant lean over low to have a good look at the fight, and as he was standing on the side of Mr Schmidt, his enormous face loomed like a brilliant sun shining straight into Mr Popov's eyes. Well, Mr Schmidt's first punch landed on Mr Popov's jaw before Mr Popov had even seen the smile on Baby Samuel's face. Mr Popov would not have fared better if he had seen the smile, because Baby Samuel only smiled *for* his friends, and Mr Schmidt was his friend, not Mr Popov. Although Mr Popov, with a very sore jaw, collected himself and tried to face Mr Schmidt again, Baby Samuel winked and moved his sun-like face, and again it was too much of, both an attraction, and a distraction, and the second blow from Mr Schmidt, unseen, landed heavily, staggering Mr Popov. Well, by the sixth blow Mr Popov was no longer able to stay on his feet, and Mr

Schmidt was declared the outright winner by Baby Samuel, who had an enormous grin on his enormous face.

And that made a very good finale for a very good birthday party, and everybody was happy as they left to go home. Well, almost everybody, because Mr Popov was not only in pain, and could hardly walk home, he was so humiliated in front of his friends of the 'ring' and he knew he would no longer be so important in VillageAll.

And although Mr Popov's body soon recovered, his spirits remained low because all his friends abandoned the 'Unique Side Show Ring', and he had to close the club very soon after the birthday party.

But for Mr Schmidt, the story was different.

After Baby Samuel's birthday party Mr Schmidt became a very important person in all of VillageAll. And Mr Hofmann, his cousin, now became very friendly and accepted an offer to live together with the Schmidts. The Pompidous and the Luigis also offered to give the Schmidts much bigger rooms in New House. Mr Schmidt, who already had a big smith shop, now enlarged it and put in it many new machines and equipment so that in VillageAll there was now two very large smith shops, the Watanabes' and the Schmidts', and both were famous and together had the best ironware in VillageAll.

Baby Samuel felt happy after his birthday party. He felt he was on top of the world. Well, he was, literally, since he was six times as large as anybody and everybody in the whole of VillageAll. He was happy to have many friends, mostly good friends, and his baby mind was tickled pink to see Mr Popov getting a good beating by his friend, Mr Schmidt.

But Baby Samuel also felt that after his birthday party he had stopped growing bigger.

He was a little puzzled. Because in Baby Samuel's baby mind, you have to grow bigger in order to grow up. And although he knew that he was already very big, he didn't feel that he was already grown-up. And nor did anybody else in VillageAll. After all, Baby Samuel was just a baby. A two-year-old baby is just a baby, even if he was a giant baby.

Everybody in VillageAll expected Baby Samuel to continue to *grow up*, even though nobody cared for him to grow *bigger*. Well, almost nobody, because Mr Smith, after Mrs Smith had said he ought to get a lot of rest, was relying more and more on Baby Samuel to do things for him, and the bigger Baby Samuel grew, the better he could rely on him. And as long as Baby Samuel was big enough to do things for him, Mr Smith didn't care whether Baby Samuel was growing up or not.

Although Mr Popov had closed his famous club after Baby Samuel's birthday party, and no longer wanted to do any 'side shows', his friend, Mr Chen, who, besides Mr Popov himself, had been the most important member of the old 'ring', told him that although, like Mr Popov, he no longer wanted to do 'side shows' about how bad

Baby Samuel was, he, Mr Chen, still wanted to continue being a member of the club even after it closed, because he liked being in a club, and there was no other club he really liked.

Unlike Mr Popov, Mr Chen had enjoyed Baby Samuel's birthday party, and had felt that having all his children in the party, who, incidentally, filled up every space of Baby Samuel's house so guests bumped into a Chen wherever they went, made him more important in VillageAll than he had ever been.

Because Mr Chen wanted to continue to be a member of Mr Popov's old club, and also because he wanted to become even more important in VillageAll, Mr Chen decided to make his own club. And Mr Chen decided that all his family would join his new club, and that his family was big enough that there was no need for anymore members for the club. Mr Chen called the new club the 'Pink Ray Club'[73] because, he said, pink was the colour of dawn, and his club would start the period when the Chens were very important in VillageAll.

The people of VillageAll, especially those who bumped into a Chen at Baby Samuel's birthday party, thought the 'Pink Ray Club' was a good idea because there were so many Chens, little Chens, medium Chens and large Chens, that it was much easier to deal with them when they were all in the same club. Mr Chen didn't only think it was easier this way, but also necessary. Mr Chen wanted to put all the strengths of the Chens together so they could do very important things in VillageAll, similar to the things that Baby Samuel was doing. Although Mr Chen's family was very big, there were no giants in it. But Mr Chen neither wanted to have a giant Chen, nor thought it was necessary because, Mr Chen said, "You either have a family or you have a giant; you cannot have both." Mr Chen also said that a big family all belonging to the same club can do all the things that Baby Samuel could do.

Well, almost all, because even Mr Chen knew that there were still things only giants could do.

After starting his new club, Mr Chen organised his family, the members of the club, so they all became even busier and the 'Pink Ray Club' became very famous in VillageAll. Everybody in VillageAll wanted to visit the Chens and look at their 'club', and many people started asking the Chens to help them do things.

The 'Pink Ray Club' had many shops and opened a new smith shop, which, Mr Chen said, would be much larger than Mr Watanabe's and Mr Schmidt's smith shops but would be different. Mr Chen's smith shop became very popular in VillageAll because although everybody liked buying implements and ironware in Mr Watanabe's and Mr Schmidt's shops, many people found that Mr Chen's smith shop sold small and cheap implements, which they needed, and which they could not get in the other two shops, and Baby Samuel said he could get some very large implements in Mr Chen's shop only because there were so many Chens who were organised by Mr Chen to use their energy and work together to make the biggest implements that ever existed!

A few months after Mr Chen started his 'club' the Chens were already helping people in VillageAll to fix things only Baby Samuel could fix before, like fixing the leaking ducts of the water aqueduct system that helped to share rainwater across all three fields of VillageAll.

CHAPTER XXI

The year following Baby Samuel's second birthday party, people in VillageAll were feeling good because they still had good memories of the party. And when it was time for the rains to come everybody thought the rains would be plenty and much better than the previous years when it only rained over Middle Field and Far Field, and only just enough for the aqueduct system to prevent another disaster crop in First Field.

So people waited for the rains with smiles on their faces.

And they waited as the smiles got thinner.

But finally no rain came.

Well, hardly any. It rained a little over Far Field, and then a little over First Field.

There was not enough rain. And because of the aqueduct system, there was not enough rain anywhere in VillageAll. Baby Samuel's farms in First Field and New Field had no corn or vegetables, and little milk to sell to shops in VillageAll.

Baby Samuel knew he would soon get hungry. And with his giant appetite, Baby Samuel hated to get hungry.

Which is why he always had ideas when hunger was the biggest thing on his mind. And this time Baby Samuel's idea was to take water from the river to the farms and fields. But Baby Samuel didn't know how it was possible to do this because the fields were so far from the river, and on ground higher than the river.

Baby Samuel talked to Mr Smith, told him his idea and asked for his advice on how to carry it out. Mr Smith was very happy to give Baby Samuel advice because Mr Smith was clever and he always had things he wanted Baby Samuel to do for him. Mr Smith advised Baby Samuel to build a noria waterwheel and an aqueduct to take the water from the river to the fields. But, Mr Smith said, the noria had to be very, very, very big so that it could lift the water high enough for the aqueduct to get it to the fields.

Well, nothing grabbed Baby Samuel's attention like the word 'big'. With tiny people around him, using tiny things that gave him a lot of trouble to handle or even to see properly, Baby Samuel was happiest when he had to deal with big things, the bigger the better.

Baby Samuel decided he was going to build an enormous noria waterwheel and aqueducts on both sides of the river.

As people in First End were telling each other how awful it was that rain didn't fall, and Mr Pompidou saying to his wife that Mr Smith really ought to ask Baby Samuel to do something about it, and Mrs Pompidou saying she could not agree more, Baby

Samuel was rushing up and down The StreetAll, talking to Mr Schmidt, Mr Watanabe and Mr Chen about how best to make an enormous waterwheel and the things he needed from their smith shops.

Having dashed up and down The StreetAll in a whirlwind of activity, Baby Samuel decided he would build the big waterwheel with wood and would fasten big buckets on either side so the water could be emptied into ducts going either side of the river. Baby Samuel asked the three smiths to make the buckets, which had to be bigger than any buckets they had ever made, and which they had to make very quickly because Baby Samuel, once started, didn't have the patience to wait!

Baby Samuel then talked to Mr Pompidou, and to his other friends in First End, Middle End and Far End, to tell them about his idea.

Everybody thought Baby Samuel had a great idea.

Well, almost everybody. Because although everybody thought that Baby Samuel's idea would save the crops of VillageAll that year and every year after that, and that Baby Samuel would not get hungry ever again, some people in Middle End said that Baby Samuel had too big an appetite, and if he continued to get bigger he would be the only one in VillageAll not to get hungry ever again.

Baby Samuel didn't like waiting, so, even as he talked to his friends, he had started preparations for building his new machine, because, anyway, Baby Samuel was only going to hear the yeses of his friends and only see their admiring faces. Well, he was just a baby and babies have no patience and only understand nods and smiles.

After ordering the buckets and fasteners and other things from the VillageAll big smith shops, Baby Samuel went about collecting timber from the far away woods in New End on the other side of the river. He would set off every morning and return by midday with huge bundles of felled trees, which he would dump by his house.

Baby Samuel chose a spot by the river, close to his giant house, and while the three smiths were working on the buckets, he set up a timber yard to cut the trees and prepare the timber he needed.

Mr Watanabe was the first of the three smiths to deliver buckets. Mr Watanabe had decided to make his buckets from wood because, he said, wooden buckets were best for carrying the most water, and considering how big they were, they looked more like barrels than buckets.

Mr Schmidt was next, and he had decided to make his buckets from clay and leather because, Mr Schmidt said, clay and leather buckets were best for making the water taste good. But considering that clay can easily break, only half of Mr Schmidt's buckets were delivered without a hole.

Mr Chen was last with his buckets, and he had decided to make iron buckets because, Mr Chen said, iron buckets were strongest, and anyway he had neither enough wood nor enough clay or leather to make big buckets. Mr Chen's buckets were quite big, and because they were made from iron, quite heavy.

Soon it was time to start putting everything together, and with his enormous size and even more enormous energy and speed, the spot where Baby Samuel was working looked as if it was struck by a hurricane that enveloped him and moved with him wherever he went. People stood a long way away to watch, and nobody dared get close enough to see what Baby Samuel was actually doing. Now and then Baby Samuel would dash, with the hurricane still enveloping him, up or down The StreetAll to collect something he had needed from Mr Watanabe's, or Mr Chen's or Mr Schmidt's shop.

Soon the people of First End, through the hurricane of Baby Samuel's movements, could make out the shape of a giant wheel. The wheel was still on its side, spread over a huge area and blocking part of The StreetAll, and because it was so big Baby Samuel's hurricane would be at one end of it while the other end was calm and clear for the eye to see the shape. But until the buckets were attached, the giant wheel remained a mystery wheel to the many onlookers.

Attaching the buckets was no easy task, especially for Baby Samuel. Because although the buckets were all big enough for him to handle, they were all different. The wooden buckets were very big and very light. The clay and leather buckets were smaller and quite heavy, and many had holes. The iron buckets were the smallest but heaviest of all. And because Baby Samuel wanted to attach buckets on both sides of the wheel, it was necessary to think carefully which bucket to attach where so the wheel would not be too heavy on one side or one end, or have too much water to lift one turn and too little to lift another turn. But Baby Samuel was just a baby, and babies do not think carefully, about anything.

So the hurricane of Baby Samuel would attach all the buckets and then try to stand the wheel, only to find it was twisting or groaning or leaning to one side. And Baby Samuel would detach all the buckets and attach them differently, and try again. After many tries, and big grunts and waving of arms every time a try failed, Baby Samuel finally found a combination which he thought would make the wheel work properly. He laid the completed wheel on its side and continued his hurricane of activity as he built the aqueducts and supports. Baby Samuel had to build two aqueducts, one on either side of the river. He used bricks and stone to build two large bases at the water's edge and then made ducts with flat wooden planks. The aqueduct to the three fields was quite long so he used timber supports, and brick bases at intervals to support the timber structure. The aqueduct to New Field was not so long and a timber structure was enough.

Bit by bit, first the people of First End, and then of Middle End and then of Far End began to understand what Baby Samuel was building: a noria waterwheel and aqueduct to save the crops!

When Baby Samuel finished the aqueduct and then stood the enormous wheel to check it against the structure, people in First End were amazed and stood in awe, and many people came to see the works from Middle End and Far End, and everybody said how clever Baby Samuel was. Well, almost everybody, because Mrs Pompidou and Mrs Schmidt said the waterwheel looked more like a Baby Samuel waterwheel, and not a VillageAll waterwheel because who, besides Baby Samuel, could make it turn and bring water to the crops?

But the crops needed the water, said Mrs Smith, and Baby Samuel was the only one so clever to have such an idea, and the only one who was big enough to make the idea work, and anyway, Baby Samuel was such a good baby to work so hard for the whole of VillageAll. And almost all Mrs Smith's neighbours agreed!

In order to set the waterwheel in its place on the river, Baby Samuel had to make good foundations. The waterwheel was so big that it had to stand in the middle of the river, where the water flowed fastest. Baby Samuel had never made foundations for a waterwheel in a river, any river, not where the water flowed slowest, nor where it flowed fastest.

And nor had anybody else in VillageAll, nor could anybody else in VillageAll ever have imagined doing such a thing; only a giant baby who could stand in the middle of the river with the water hardly coming up to his waist could ever think of doing something like that.

Well, Baby Samuel didn't waste any time thinking about what he had to do because babies don't like thinking.

Baby Samuel just took big timber poles and a special big mallet that Mr Schmidt made for him and walked into the river and started to hammer the poles into the riverbed. Baby Samuel needed a lot of poles to make strong foundations for a platform on either side of the waterwheel. The platforms also had to support the troughs at the end of the aqueducts. But with his speed and energy he soon had the platforms built and was ready to mount the huge waterwheel. The poles that made up the foundations looked and felt very strong, but nobody knew, nor for now wanted to know, what would happen if the river flowed faster or slower, or if the water rose or fell.

Baby Samuel stood the huge waterwheel up and started to move with it into the river in order to install it in place.

Although Baby Samuel was a giant baby, he had made a giant waterwheel, with giant buckets, and it was a giant struggle to carry it through the water. Onlookers in The StreetAll stood frozen to the ground as they stared breathlessly at the giant baby and the giant wheel butting against each other, lurching together one way and then the other, and moving step by unsteady step into the river.

Baby Samuel finally reached the platforms he had built in the middle of the river, and with a Herculean effort, and a grunt that sounded like a short burst of fireworks, he placed the waterwheel on its supports. Baby Samuel then had to climb on top of one of the platforms to secure the waterwheel shaft in place, which provided the onlookers with another heart-stopping moment, as although the platform looked large and strong for the waterwheel, it didn't look large or strong enough for Baby Samuel *and* the waterwheel together. But, apart from a slight wobble of the platform as Baby Samuel hauled himself up and climbed on top, he had no more trouble as he fixed the wheel and then anchored it with a rope to stop it from turning while he finished the aqueduct.

Baby Samuel then resumed his hurricane-like activity to make two troughs, where the water would pour from the buckets, on either side of the wheel, and then made ducts to connect them with the aqueduct bases at the riverbanks.

Once it was all finished, Baby Samuel stood back to admire his work. The onlookers had by this time swelled into a very large crowd, with almost all the people of First End now watching.

Baby Samuel gestured to the onlookers who ringed the site of the works, still strewn with bits of timber, tools and bits of iron, pins, screws and nails, and smiled his broad amiable smile and just said, "Waterwheel."

This, for Baby Samuel, concluded the inauguration ceremony of the project. Well, he was just a baby and babies are not good at ceremonies.

Baby Samuel walked straight into the waters of the river and to the middle where the waterwheel stood, and unceremoniously cut the rope that anchored the giant wheel.

At first nothing happened as the large crowd of VillageAll people held their breaths. Then, creaking, murmuring and groaning, the huge wheel began to stir as the rushing water was pushing on the paddles that went deep in the river. Slowly the wheel started to turn, and the first buckets, full of water, started to climb up the side. Baby Samuel remained in the water by the wheel to make sure the wheel would turn properly. As more buckets emerged from the water and the wheel now had to lift more and more weight all the way to the top, it seemed to hesitate and slow again. At which moment, Baby Samuel gave it a push to encourage it to gather speed. Baby Samuel had to give the giant waterwheel a few more pushes before it gathered enough momentum to keep turning. Meanwhile, the buckets were emptying all their water into the two troughs. Well, almost all their water, because there was so much splashing, and water seemed to shower and drip everywhere. But it seemed that enough water collected in the troughs so a stream began moving in either direction towards the aqueducts.

At that there was a simultaneous burst of applause from VillageAll people watching, and everybody felt so happy and proud of Baby Samuel. Well, almost everybody, because Mrs Pompidou said to Mrs Schmidt, who happened to be standing beside her, that, "Really, Baby Samuel is always in such a hurry when he is worried about getting hungry and, really, he should have consulted with Mr Pompidou about the best way to build the waterwheel and aqueducts because only Mr Pompidou knows what such things should look like."

Well, Mrs Smith heard this conversation and was quite angry and said to Mrs Luigi, Mrs De Graff and Mrs Cortez, who happened to be standing beside her, that the whole people of VillageAll had better be happy because Baby Samuel had got rid of worry about the years without rain and well, if the waterwheel or the aqueducts break down then Baby Samuel would always be there to fix them, wouldn't he?

Baby Samuel's noria waterwheel saved the crops that year, and the bakers, grocers and butchers of VillageAll were happy again because they had plenty to sell, and plenty of customers to sell to.

And everybody in VillageAll was happy because they didn't have to worry about getting hungry again, not this year, nor any year after this year. Well, almost everybody, because, unlike Baby Samuel and his friends, some poor people, like the family of Mr Ndiaye, knew that they would still be hungry, even after the giant waterwheel brought the water to nourish the crops of VillageAll.

The giant waterwheel would sometimes stop, and Baby Samuel would go in the river and get it to turn again. But this didn't worry anybody in VillageAll because it was so easy for Baby Samuel to keep the wheel turning.

CHAPTER XXII

Soon after Baby Samuel's noria waterwheel made the people of VillageAll happy and not worried anymore about the rains, something strange happened in VillageAll.

People started to notice smells in the air, not very nice smells. At first the smells were not strong and everybody believed they would soon go away and the air would be nice again, as before. But, instead, the smells started to get stronger.

It was a bit strange, everybody would say, because, well, the smells were like the smell of farts, people's farts, everybody's farts!

At first everybody said that the smell was coming from somebody else's house, and nobody said that *they* were making smells. But as the smells increased and people smelled them everywhere and every day, it became more difficult to blame somebody else, and soon everybody understood that the smells were coming from *everybody's* house. But the strongest smells came from the big houses of First End and New End, especially from Baby Samuel's house.

Some people had said, even before Baby Samuel's second birthday party, that sometimes when they passed his house they noticed bad smells coming out of the house. But nobody worried about that because Baby Samuel was just a baby, and babies sometimes make awful smells.

But now everybody noticed. Because although every house was making smells, the smells from Baby Samuel's house were filling the air all over First End and parts of Middle and Far Ends. Well, a giant baby farts giant farts, and giant farts make giant smelly winds that travel far afield, as well as noises that can be heard at the other end of VillageAll. Soon people passing in The StreetAll in front of Baby Samuel's house would cover their noses and hurry past, and would dive for cover if they heard the booming noise of a Baby Samuel fart, because such a noise would announce a new cloud of smells soon to envelop The StreetAll.

Nobody knew why people were farting more than before or why their farts were more smelly than before, because although some people had a little bit of indigestion or stomach ache, nobody was really ill and everybody was as happy as before. Well, almost as happy as before. Because having those smells every day made people a little unhappy and made them wonder how they could stop the smells.

Mrs Smith said that it was because people were eating too much, because now there was always plenty of food, and made Mr Smith tell everybody that the Smiths would start to eat less food. Everybody agreed with Mrs Smith and said they would eat less. Well, almost everybody, because Mrs Pompidou said that eating too much only made you fat, and that eating badly was what made people fart. Although everybody could not agree if it was eating too much or eating badly that was causing the problem, everybody agreed that whatever it was, Baby Samuel should stop doing it, because it was the smells from Baby Samuel's house that were the strongest. But how can anybody tell Baby Samuel to stop doing anything?

Especially to stop making bad smells?

And even more especially when Baby Samuel said he didn't smell any bad smells?

So, everybody in First End gave up on the idea of talking to Baby Samuel about his smelly farting, and said they would instead pray for a strong wind to blow his smells over the river and away from The StreetAll.

Well, almost everybody, because Mrs Smith, forgetting to feel like a close friend rather than his mother, said that Mr Smith would talk to Baby Samuel. Now Mr Smith liked to talk to Baby Samuel, but not about bad smells, and especially not about Baby Samuel's bad smells. But since upsetting Baby Samuel was still much better than upsetting Mrs Smith, he promptly went to Baby Samuel's house to talk to him.

Baby Samuel's house was quite smelly, but not as smelly as Mr Smith had worried it would be. It seemed that most of the fart smells went out of the windows, across The StreetAll and to the houses on the other side.

As he always did when Mr Smith visited him, Baby Samuel lifted Mr Smith and sat him on a high chair that he made specially for him so he could see him while talking to him in his house. While Baby Samuel was in a playful and chatty mood, Mr Smith was nervous and was not sure how to start the conversation about farts and smells. He could only think about what Mrs Smith had said about eating too much, so he suddenly said to Baby Samuel, "You know, old chap, you really need to eat less." And that, precisely, was all Mr Smith had to say to instantly wipe the smile off Baby Samuel's face.

Baby Samuel was a giant baby with a giant appetite, and ever since he was one month old his life was a struggle to satisfy his appetite and keep hunger away. Hunger was Baby Samuel's biggest enemy, and also his best friend when he found new ideas to get rid of it! So, to be told to eat less, and by Mr Smith himself, was not only unexpected, but very confusing and quite upsetting.

Baby Samuel scratched his head, as he tended to do when he was faced with a complicated situation or a question he didn't understand, which was not very unusual, and made a couple of grunts, which, although not really loud for Baby Samuel, could be heard a long way down The StreetAll. Mr Smith, who knew Baby Samuel well, and knew the signs of Baby Samuel starting to get upset, felt his own nerves fraying, and his mouth drying, but felt, nevertheless, that he had to press on as he had not yet mentioned anything about smells. So Mr Smith added, "Well, you know it is the smelly farts and all that." And that, precisely, was all Mr Smith had to say to bring on Baby Samuel's headache in an instant. The kind of headache Baby Samuel got when he heard babies crying. Because even though Baby Samuel knew he was just a baby, he didn't like anybody to tell him he was a baby, and especially not to tell him that he farted and made smells like babies.

When Baby Samuel got that babies-crying type of headache he often did terrible things. But this time there was only poor Mr Smith, on the special high chair, in front of him, and he could not very well do anything to him, so he just let out a short yell of, "My head," which was quite loud, even for Baby Samuel, and dashed out of his house heading towards the river, with a smelly cloud following in his wake.

The short yell from Baby Samuel had rattled Mr Smith and made his teeth chatter slightly, while his hands tightened their grip even more on the arms of his high chair before he suddenly found himself alone. Baby Samuel had not put a ladder on the chair because, well, Mr Smith would only ever sit on the chair in his presence, wouldn't he?

So, Mr Smith, still somewhat shaken and upset, had to find a way to get down. He didn't want to shout for help, in case the Pompidous heard him before Mrs Smith did. He had no choice but to slide down one of the chair legs. It was somewhat undignified and a little dangerous, considering his age, and he was lucky not only to come down without falling and injuring himself, but also to come down without anybody seeing him!

But although nobody saw Mr Smith's undignified climb down from his special high chair, those who saw him sneaking out of Baby Samuel's house, with head bent down and feet shuffling unsteadily, having seen Baby Samuel's rather dramatic exit, could tell that on that day Mr Smith didn't have a very enjoyable visit with Baby Samuel.

After the incident of the visit of Mr Smith, people said that if Mr Smith could not talk to Baby Samuel about farting and smells, well, then, nobody could talk to him, and that Baby Samuel would continue to fart and make smells and everybody had to live with that. But everybody had to live with smells coming out of all the other houses of VillageAll. Especially now that not only the big houses of First End, but some houses in Far End were also making quite a lot of smells.

For some time their neighbours had been bothered by a lot of smells coming from the Chens' house. And people said, well, the Chens were such a big family, and it was because of all the hard work that the members of the 'Pink Ray Club' were doing. But Mrs Watanabe said people didn't fart because of hard work: it was rather that smelly farts in the neighbourhood made working very hard!

And more recently still it was the Singhs' house that started to make more and more smells. Well, the Singh family was almost as big as the Chen family, even if they didn't have a club of their own.

After the incident of the visit of Mr Smith, Mrs Smith was angry with him because he not only failed to stop Baby Samuel farting, but also made him angry. But although Mrs Smith gave up on talking to Baby Samuel, she wanted to stop other houses in VillageAll making big smells. Mrs Smith talked to Mrs Schmidt and asked her for help, and Mrs Schmidt had an idea: she said that together with their friends the women should make a special club to make VillageAll less smelly. Mrs Schmidt said she would talk to Mrs Andersson, Mrs Pompidou and Mrs Watanabe and ask them to help in making the club.

Soon First End heard about the new club, and later all of VillageAll heard about it.

The women called their new club the 'Gas Promise' club[74] because members of the club would talk to every family in VillageAll to make them promise to fart less.

CHAPTER XXIII

The 'Gas Promise' club was doing a good job and although there was still a lot of smells in VillageAll, the smells were not getting worse, and the smells made VillageAll seem a little smaller because they were the same in First End, Middle End or Far End.

Although people in VillageAll didn't like the smells, everybody thought that if Baby Samuel had big meals and made big smells then it was all right to make *some* smells if they too wanted to have big meals. Well, almost everybody, because some people said that you could have big meals without making any smells, but nobody knew how to do that!

People also didn't know how they could *eat* big meals like Baby Samuel's meals. Because, although everybody had a big appetite and wanted to eat a big meal, nobody had a big stomach like Baby Samuel's. To have a big stomach like Baby Samuel's you had to be as big as Baby Samuel!

So, everybody in VillageAll wanted to be as big as Baby Samuel.

Well, almost everybody, because Mrs Pompidou said to her husband that being so big was gross and "think how VillageAll would look like if everybody was as big as Baby Samuel." Mr Pompidou said he could not agree more but that it might not be a bad thing if one was just a little more like Baby Samuel! Mr Pompidou said that, after all, Mr & Mrs Smith think and act as if they are quite as big as Baby Samuel.

Well, people in VillageAll, especially in Middle End and Far End, did want to be as big as Baby Samuel. But, although nobody in VillageAll could *really* be as big as Baby Samuel, everybody could *pretend* to be as big. Soon, many strange houses started to appear in Middle End and Far End because some people changed their houses to make them look a little like Baby Samuel's house. Some houses had very large windows sticking above the roof, and some houses had enormous front doors that could not be closed. Some houses had no windows, because Baby Samuel blocked all windows which looked out on the river because he said the river reminded him of the Nomans and he didn't want to remember the Nomans. And some houses even had a crooked roof because Baby Samuel built his house in a hurry and part of the roof didn't fit well!

But not only houses, because some people started wearing shoes that were much larger than their feet so they had to tie their feet to the shoes with rope so they did not come off while they walked. And some people in Middle End and Far End just wanted to give their houses and clothes the same colour or shape but not the same size as Baby Samuel's.

After a while, VillageAll started to look somewhat alike wherever you went, and Mrs Smith was very pleased whenever she passed a house in Middle End that looked like houses in First End or New End, and wondered why Far End still looked like Far End and not more like First End or New End.

"That is all very well," said Mrs Pompidou to her husband, "but look at those grotesque houses and people." Mr Pompidou said it could not be helped because pretending made you feel bigger and stronger and, after all, Baby Samuel liked to see people imitating him. Baby Samuel was just a baby and babies feel loved when you imitate them.

CHAPTER XXIV

Mr Moschel and Baby Samuel were now very good friends, and Baby Samuel liked to visit Mr Moschel and talk to him. They would walk together around the back woods of Middle End and sit under trees to chat. Well, anyway, it was *like* walking together, because nobody could walk together with a giant baby.

One early autumn day Baby Samuel was rushing up The StreetAll doing his News Imp job. As he passed by Middle End he slowed to see if Mr Mustapha or Mr Moschel had, or wanted, any news. Mr Mustapha was busy in his shop, and only Mr Moschel was about.

Mr Moschel told Baby Samuel that he had news about a hornets' nest in the backyard of Mr Mustapha's house, and said that he had never in his life seen such enormous hornets and he was worried in case they attacked him. Mr Moschel then offered to show Baby Samuel the nest.

Baby Samuel followed Mr Moschel to the back of the house. Mr Moschel entered the yard through the back door while Baby Samuel stepped with one big foot over the wall. There was room for only one of Baby Samuel's big feet inside the yard. Mr Moschel then pointed up to the roof edge, and there, under the eaves was what looked like a big muddy ball stuck to the wall. There was a small hole near the bottom, and big hornets were flying in and out through the hole. Well, they were only big if, like everybody else, you were standing five feet above the ground, but for a giant baby they were like tiny specks of dust, which he could hardly see, and Baby Samuel was wondering what Mr Moschel was making a fuss about! Without saying anything, Baby Samuel bent down to see the nest more closely, and then just swiped at it with his big hand in order to get it off the wall and make it fall to the ground so he could stamp on it with his enormous feet.

But the nest broke in half. One half remained stuck to the wall, and the other half fell to the ground. The hornets, who had had nothing to do with, and would want nothing to do with Baby Samuel, and whom Baby Samuel could hardly even see, didn't know exactly what had happened, except that they were now forced out of their home by an enemy, and, therefore, that they were very, very angry. In order to survive, the hornets had to attack their enemy, and in order to attack their enemy they had to find it. So the hornets were now flying in a state of great agitation, sensing the air for smells that would give them clues for what to attack.

Mr Moschel, who had had wasp and hornet stings before, didn't want to be amongst angry hornets, any-more than they wanted him to be amongst them, and so immediately rushed indoors. As he was getting in, Mr Moschel shouted to his giant friend to beware the nasty hornets. Mr Moschel didn't think that you could win a battle with hornets, even if you were a giant like Baby Samuel, but he thought that it was better that Baby Samuel discovered that by himself; it would be a surer way of getting rid of hornets' nests in future.

Meanwhile, the angry hornets were buzzing all round Baby Samuel and it was not long before they sensed the smell of their nest on his hand and they all at once headed for the enemy.

Baby Samuel was at first bemused by the little cloud of flyers buzzing around him, but the first sting on his hand jolted him slightly and he thought he didn't like those tiny flying creatures, so he shook them off his hand and started waving his arms in the air to try to dispel them. The waving of his 'smelly' hand was taken by the hornets, who were in a life and death war, to be a new attack and made their own attacks more frenzied, and this time a bunch of them headed to Baby Samuel's big nose and by the time he had noticed them they had each one of them stung him many times[75].

A hornet's sting is painful. It is very painful on the nose, and very, very painful if many hornets sting at the same time, and very, very, very painful for a giant baby who had always been too big to be stung by a hornet, or by anything else.

As Baby Samuel felt the pain he became very angry and his head started aching. Very soon the headache grew fiercer and became that baby-crying type of headache, and, with the hornets still buzzing around him,

Baby Samuel could not help aiming a mighty kick at the wall at the top of which still remained one half of the nest of some very angry hornets. The kick was followed by another and another, and by punches from his huge fists to any remaining walls and ceilings around that area of the house.

While Baby Samuel was busy venting his anger on the walls of Mr Mustapha's house, he didn't hear the screams, yells and wailing of the people inside. Well, Baby Samuel didn't really want to hear any yelling because it would only make his headache worse, and then he would become even angrier. So Baby Samuel didn't look inside to see how many children were hurt, or how badly they were hurt, or whether Mrs Mustapha was hurt. And after a last kick, Baby Samuel left, clutching a now very red and very swollen nose, and, with hornets trailing after him, headed to his house to nurse both his stung nose and his bad headache.

Mr Mustapha, meanwhile, had heard the sounds of crashing walls, followed by the screams, and had ran back home to find that the falling walls had crushed the legs of one of his daughters, and that two others of his children were badly cut and bruised. Mrs Mustapha was also badly hurt in the face as masonry fell on her when she rushed to move the children to safety.

Of course Mr Mustapha had not known what happened, but he thought he saw the shadow of a smirk on Mr Moschel's face as he looked out of his room on the other side of the house, which, of course, was not affected at all. Mr Mustapha could not help feeling that, somehow, Mr Moschel must have had something to do with the tragedy that befell his house.

Baby Samuel's big red nose was very big news in VillageAll. Nobody had ever seen such a huge nose before. And everybody in VillageAll thought that the bigger the nose the more painful it must have been. And everybody felt so sorry for Baby Samuel.

Well, almost everybody, because Mr Mustapha's neighbours didn't think that it was Baby Samuel who needed, or deserved the sympathy. And after more people saw what happened to Mr Mustapha's house and his family they also started to feel less sorry for Baby Samuel and his sore nose.

When Mr Smith heard about Baby Samuel and the hornets, he was angry with the hornets and sorry for Baby Samuel. He said to Mrs Smith that the hornets behaved badly, and Baby Samuel was only trying to help his friends in Middle End. Mr Smith said he wanted to go with Mr Pompidou to Middle End to see if any hornets' nests remained because he was worried about his friend, Mr Moschel. Mrs Smith said that Mr Smith had better be worried about the Mustaphas after what Baby Samuel did, and that going to Middle End would neither make the Mustaphas or the Moschels happy, nor make the hornets behave better.

But Mr Smith decided to go and talk to Mr Pompidou. When he arrived at the Pompidous' Mr Cortez was visiting, so Mr Smith asked both Mr Pompidou and Mr Cortez to go with him to Middle End.

But Mrs Pompidou said that it was not a good idea and that 'one red nose is enough'. Mr Smith said that Baby Samuel's giant round nose was an easy and appealing target for badly-behaved hornets, but his and Mr Pompidou's and Mr Cortez's are neither big nor appealing, and, anyway, he knew how to deal with badly behaving hornets. But Mrs Pompidou said that Mr Smith rather should find out how hornets deal with badly behaving people, and said that whether Mr Pompidou's nose was appealing or not she would rather keep it away from the hornets, and so Mr Pompidou had better stay home.

And so Mr Smith and Mr Cortez went together, without Mr Pompidou, and well, Mr Smith was quite wrong about both his nose and the hornets. When Mr Smith and Mr Cortez approached the damaged house of the Mustaphas, they could still see hornets buzzing in agitation, looking for their enemy. Mr Smith and Mr Cortez wanted to look for more nests around the house so they tried to keep away from the buzzing hornets as they took small careful steps. But before they could get far, a couple of hornets came to sniff the air around them. Mr Smith, who earlier was full of courage and said that his nose was safe from the hornets, started to wave his arms in panic at the hornets. Sensing a battle, the hornets now took much more interest and called their mates for help. Soon Mr Smith and Mr Cortez were both waving their arms in panic trying to fend off the determined hornets. It was not long before both Mr Smith's and Mr Cortez's hands were in contact with the flying hornets. Now the hornets had the scent of another enemy, and they set in hot pursuit as both Mr Smith and Mr Cortez ran away from the Mustaphas' home. Mr Smith's nose may not have been very appealing, but to an avenging hornet it was all it needed and it did not hesitate[76].

When Mr Smith got home clutching his red nose, Mrs Smith was neither amused nor forgiving, even if she still offered some sympathy!

Baby Samuel's nose soon started to recover. And although it was almost back to its normal colour within a few days, the worst hornet stings left some small marks, and Baby Samuel became obsessed with big flying insects and thought that they were always after him, even when nobody could see any near him.

But although the Mustapha family could rebuild the part of their house that was destroyed, they could not rebuild the legs of their daughter, nor could they remove the bad scars on Mrs Mustapha's face, and from that day onwards they cringed every time Baby Samuel went passing by.

Mr Mustapha's neighbours in Middle End started talking about keeping Baby Samuel away from Middle End. But how can you tell a giant where to go and where not to go? Mrs Mustapha said that, well, people can't tell Baby Samuel not to come, but hornets could, so maybe they should have more hornets' nests in Middle End. She said that neither giant babies nor important people from First End liked having a red nose, so having hornets buzzing about would stop all unwelcome visitors. Mr Mustapha's neighbours all agreed with Mrs Mustapha.

Well, almost all, because Mr Moschel did not like hornets and did like visitors from First End and, most of all, wanted Baby Samuel to keep visiting Middle End. But Mr Moschel knew that sometimes it is better to be quiet: if the Mustaphas and their neighbours became less friendly with Baby Samuel and First End people, then Baby Samuel and First End people would be even more friendly with him!

People in VillageAll, especially in Middle End and First End, started to see hornets more often than before. All hornets remembered scents, but these were a special breed of hornets which had very, very long memories, especially of certain scents.

CHAPTER XXV

After the hornets' nest incident Baby Samuel started to behave strangely. He was often in a bad mood, especially when he passed through Middle End, and he would shout at anybody he met and sometimes even kick a tree or a wall. Baby Samuel didn't mean to break things with these kicks but even though he was just a baby, he was a giant baby with giant feet so even the smallest of his kicks made a lot of damage and made people feel bad. The people of Middle End didn't think that Baby Samuel didn't like them anymore, but they thought that he was behaving as if he didn't. So the people of Middle End felt bad both about the damage of Baby Samuel's kicks and about feeling he didn't like them.

But the very next day, Baby Samuel would be in a very happy mood and would be helpful to everybody he met, and he would forget completely what he did the previous day.

One day, when Baby Samuel was in a very bad mood and after he upset many people in Middle End, he met Mr Pompidou in First End. Mr Pompidou was of course Baby Samuel's friend so was worried about the bad feelings of people in Middle End. Mr Pompidou said to Baby Samuel that since he was such a big baby he should behave less like a baby and more like a big boy. Well, although Baby Samuel was very, very big, he didn't know the difference between a big baby and a big boy, or how a big boy should behave, so Baby Samuel didn't understand what Mr Pompidou said, but like a baby, got very angry and shouted at his friend and said he could do what he liked, and said he didn't want to talk to Mr Pompidou anymore.

But the next day, when Baby Samuel met Mr Pompidou he was all smiles, all charm, just like any baby, and he had forgotten all that happened the previous day.

Soon, people in VillageAll started saying that it was as if there were two Baby Samuels, a good one and a bad one, and if you saw Baby Samuel approaching you didn't know which of the two it was, and if it was the bad one then it was not the Baby Samuel that you wanted to meet.

And the people of VillageAll started saying to each other that it is all too well having two Baby Samuels, but if one of them was a bad one then he would ruin all the good things that the good one did for VillageAll. Most of all, the people of VillageAll wanted to know what changed Baby Samuel and made him behave badly some days.

It was not long before Mrs Pompidou said to her husband, "Why, I think Mrs Smith ought to send the bad

Baby Samuel back to where she got him from!" but Mr Pompidou said that a bad Baby Samuel for VillageAll was still a good Baby Samuel for Mrs Smith.

One day while Mr Smith and Mr Pompidou were visiting Baby Samuel in his house to have a chat with him, Baby Samuel suddenly said to them, "Why is everybody so small and slow and useless? I want friends who are big like me." Well, Mr Smith and Mr Pompidou didn't know what to say because they didn't think that everybody was small and slow and useless, and they knew even less what to say about how Baby Samuel could have giant friends like himself.

Baby Samuel said that he liked his friends in First End and that they were small but they were not useless, but he didn't any more like people in other places and that they made him angry. He said he wanted all the people of VillageAll to be like his friends in First End.

Mr Pompidou became quite still when he heard this. Mr Pompidou, remembering what Mrs Pompidou had said about the bad Baby Samuel, knew he had to be very careful about what he said so that he neither upset Baby Samuel, nor Mrs Pompidou.

But Mr Smith didn't see or hear a bad Baby Samuel: for Mr Smith there was only the one Baby Samuel, who could be a little naughty sometimes. So Mr Smith said that anyway people of Middle End and Far End were already becoming like the people of First End and it was because of Baby Samuel and what he did for VillageAll, so he should not upset those people and instead should wait a little longer.

Baby Samuel frowned and made some strange mumbling noises: he was just a baby and babies do not understand grown-up talk, and understand even less why they have to wait for anything.

Then Baby Samuel said a very strange thing. He said that since he was the News Imp of VillageAll he got everybody's news so he knew everybody's secrets and so he could make everybody do what he wanted them to do.

And this time it was Mr Smith who frowned and made strange mumbling noises. Mr Pompidou also frowned, but was very, very quiet. Neither Mr Smith nor Mr Pompidou found anymore words to say. It didn't matter whether it was the bad Baby Samuel or the good but sometimes naughty Baby Samuel in front of them, either was the giant baby who loomed large over the whole of VillageAll.

The people of VillageAll soon heard rumours about what Baby Samuel said and they were even more sure that there were two Baby Samuels and they became even more worried about meeting the bad Baby Samuel. Especially in Middle End, people started running away and hiding in their houses every time they saw Baby Samuel coming near them, and mothers would say to their children that if they didn't behave Baby Samuel the Monster would get them.

CHAPTER XXVI

Around the time of Baby Samuel's incident with the hornets, the people of VillageAll began to notice something strange about the house of the Singh family in Far End.

Although everybody in VillageAll could see that the Singh family was very, very large, everybody could not see how such a large family lived in such a small house. People in VillageAll would joke that the Singhs must have lived on top of each other in order to fit in their small house!

But now everybody could see that the Singh family house was rising up in the air! The house was getting taller. Baby Samuel was the first to mention to his friends in First End that he thought the Singhs' house was getting higher and was, step-by-step, coming up closer to him. That is when Baby Samuel's friends began to realise that Mr Singh had started to build on top of the old house to make more room for his family. People passing through Far End started to notice how tall the Singhs' house had become. The house now rose six storeys high and so everybody believed it was the tallest building in VillageAll. Well, of course this is not including Baby Samuel's house, because everybody believed that no house in VillageAll could ever be bigger than Baby Samuel's house.

The people of VillageAll stopped joking about the Singhs living on top of each other. Because although the Singh family now truly lived on top of each other, there were so many floors that they were now living in nice big rooms and there was room for everybody.

Although the Singh family was now more comfortable, they were still poor. Mr Singh believed his children were clever and were also well behaved, so he had an idea. Mr Singh told his children that as they now had more room in their house, they should use the new rooms as their offices and they should become the clerks of the people of VillageAll; they should do their reading and writing and keep their books for them.

When the people of VillageAll heard this news they were amazed at this new idea, but everybody was happy to hear about it. Well, almost everybody, because Mrs Smith said that, of course she knew the Singh family very well, and although she didn't like doing this kind of work herself, she was not sure that the Singh family was clever enough to do this most important of work. But Mrs Smith's neighbours said they thought the Singh family was clever enough, and Mrs Pompidou said to her husband she thought that Mrs Smith should have been more careful in what she said because everybody knew that the Singh family was much cleverer than the Smiths!

Many people in VillageAll wanted the Singh family to do their paperwork and their accounts for them, and soon the Singh family became famous in all of VillageAll, and much less poor. And although the people of VillageAll didn't think that Mr & Mrs Singh's house was big, like the houses in First End, they soon started to talk about how much room there was when you added all the floors together, and Mr Pompidou said to his wife, "I do like the idea of living at the top of a tall house, like the Singhs," and Mrs Pompidou said she agreed entirely.

It was not long before everybody in VillageAll realised that the Singhs now lived in one of the biggest houses in VillageAll. Well, almost everybody, because Mrs Smith said that a big house must have a big garden, and it didn't matter how high a house was, if it didn't have a garden it was not a real house.

But, notwithstanding what Mrs Smith said, the Singh family became one of the most important families in VillageAll.

CHAPTER XXVII

Soon after the Singh family became one of the most important families in VillageAll the mysterious illness returned to VillageAll[77].

This time Baby Samuel was the first to become ill. Soon after that all the people of First End became very ill. At the same time this was happening, the crops in First Field and Far Field were not growing well because the rains were very late and there was not enough water for the crops to grow properly.

Even when people in First End were ill they were puzzled about why there was not enough water, because Baby Samuel had made the big noria wheel so that even if there was not enough rain there would always be enough water for the fields of VillageAll.

Well, the noria wheel was still working and even though the aqueducts had many leaks, there was still a lot of water running in them.

And the people of First End were asking each other, "Where is the water going?"

Although Baby Samuel was very ill he still went out to do his News Imp job for VillageAll and during his outings he explained to his friends in First End that he and Mr Smith had recently asked the Knabers to help run the waterworks of VillageAll because Baby Samuel was having a lot of trouble running it by himself and because the Knabers knew a lot about waterworks.

Well, this was big news indeed!

Because until then the Knabers were like shadows in the night that people talked about only in secret, and nobody was sure if they really existed, and if they did what they really did and how.

So although people in First End were very sick the news spread very quickly and Mr Pompidou dragged himself out of his sickbed and insisted that Mr Schmidt and Mr Luigi, and their other neighbours, also drag themselves out of their sickbeds so they could talk together about this very important news. Mr Pompidou also sent a message to Mr Watanabe and Mr Chen asking them to join the meeting. The mysterious illness in the Far End was not as bad as in First End or New End, so Mr Watanabe and Mr Chen could walk to First End to attend the men's meeting.

When the men got together they were feeling neither good nor well, but they knew they had to talk about the Knabers. But what the men knew was a lot less than what they didn't know. Did the Knabers bring the mysterious illness? Did the Knabers bring the mysterious illness the times before also? Did the Knabers have medicine for the mysterious illness? Why is there not enough water for the crops, where did the water go? Were the Knabers taking the water for themselves?

What the men did know now was that the Knabers do exist and that they somehow found out how to become friends with Baby Samuel ...

The men thought that if Baby Samuel worked with the Knabers and needed their help then VillageAll must work with the Knabers and must need their help.

The men also thought that they had better talk to Baby Samuel first before they did anything about the Knabers, so they decided that Mr Pompidou should first talk to Mr Smith to find out more about the Knabers and to find the best way to talk to Baby Samuel.

The women of First End also decided they must talk about the Knabers.

Mrs Pompidou, who was only slightly ill, called on Mrs Schmidt and asked other neighbours to join them. Mrs Cortez, Mrs Luigi and Mrs Spiros were all very ill. They didn't like to leave their sickbeds. They liked even less to go for a chat with Mrs Pompidou while they were ill. But they decided that they liked least of all to become even more ill, so they went to the meeting.

Mrs Pompidou told the women that the bad Baby Samuel asked the Knabers to help him because he thought they would bring him more food, but that the Knabers were instead taking the water away from VillageAll fields to make their own food. Mrs Pompidou also said every time the Knabers appeared in First End they brought the mysterious illness with them.

157

All the women said they agreed entirely with Mrs Pompidou.

Well, almost all, because Mrs Schmidt, who was almost fit and healthy, didn't say anything because she was worried about what Baby Samuel would feel if he heard Mrs Pompidou.

Mrs Pompidou finally said that the first thing First End had to do was to find a cure for the mysterious illness so she was going to tell Mr Pompidou to talk to the good Baby Samuel and find out if the Knabers had the medicine.

All the women agreed.

Well, almost all, because Mrs Luigi said to Mrs Cortez, who was beside her, that Mrs Pompidou was very clever but her head was in the clouds as usual. Mrs Pompidou could tell Mr Pompidou anything she liked but the Knabers were a giant problem, made by a giant baby, and who could solve the problem of a giant baby?

When Mr Pompidou called on the Smiths to consult with Mr Smith, Mrs Smith let him in and told him that Mr Smith was too ill to see him. But Mrs Smith told Mr Pompidou that she saw the Knabers when they came to see Mr Smith at night. She said that the Knabers never came out during the day because they were night creatures. Mrs Smith also said that the Knabers were giving medicine and food to Baby Samuel and that Baby Samuel should soon get well.

Mrs Smith told Mr Pompidou that she didn't much like the Knabers because although they were like people, they didn't look like nice people and because they always hid their faces so you could never see their eyes. But she said that Mr Smith told her that the Knabers were good and VillageAll needed them.

Soon after Mr Pompidou's visit to the Smiths, Baby Samuel started to get better, and Mrs Pompidou said to her husband, "I am so happy you did something about Baby Samuel's illness, if you didn't, what would have happened to Baby Samuel?"

Soon Mr Smith also started to get better after some people in First End said they saw Knabers go into the Smiths' house during the night.

Mr Pompidou, notwithstanding what his wife had said to him, knew well why only Baby Samuel and Mr Smith were getting better, but nobody else in First End.

At the same time that Baby Samuel and Mr Smith were getting better, people in Far End also started to get better, and Baby Samuel told his friends that there was enough rain in Far Field so the crops were growing well even though the aqueducts were not bringing enough water from the river. In Far End also people said they saw Knabers going into the Chens' and Watanabes' houses at night.

But in First End most people remained ill, and there was still not enough water for the crops because the rains still didn't come[78].

Although the Schmidts were quite healthy, and the Smiths had almost recovered, the Pompidous still felt unwell and the Luigis and Cortezes were still very ill, and especially the Spiros who were still very, very ill.

CHAPTER XXVIII

Baby Samuel's third birthday was now approaching.

Although many families in First End were still ill, Baby Samuel decided to have a birthday party because, as he told Mr Smith and Mr Pompidou, he felt fine and his friends, the Knabers, promised him that they would help all families in First End to get better soon.

But Baby Samuel had not completely recovered from the mysterious illness. He was also very bothered by some things: when he was running up and down The StreetAll to do his News Imp job he didn't seem to be running as fast as before; when he crossed the big river the water came up higher; sometimes he could not reach up in his house to get things on high shelves.

Could it be that Baby Samuel was getting smaller?

Well, Baby Samuel didn't want to think so because he was still a baby and wanted to grow up, but how can you grow up if you start growing smaller? So Baby Samuel thought it was the mysterious illness which made him think he was getting smaller, and if he had a big birthday party with all his friends he would get all better and he would not feel smaller anymore.

So Baby Samuel invited to his birthday party all his friends in all of VillageAll, and many more who were not his friends. He even invited, for the first time, Mr & Mrs Ndiaye who, also for the first time, were managing to look after their little garden, which was not so little anymore. Because he wanted to have a good party he also invited his friends, the Knabers, and asked them to help him prepare for the party.

Everybody in VillageAll was thrilled with the news of the party.

Well, almost everybody, because Mrs Pompidou said to her husband, "How can we have a good party with the Knabers?" Mr Pompidou said he could not agree more, but said that everybody wanted to have a party with Baby Samuel, not with each other, and not with the Knabers, so if Baby Samuel was in a good mood everybody would be happy.

Well, maybe not everybody, because Mrs Cortez and Mrs Spiros said to their husbands, "How can we enjoy the party while we are still ill?" Mr Cortez and Mr Spiros told their wives that the Knabers promised Baby Samuel to make everybody well and maybe they will give them some medicine at the party.

Although First End people were looking forward to Baby Samuel's birthday party they were worried about having enough food and drinks because even though many people were getting better there was still not enough water for First End and New End crops. So people in First End were happy when, shortly before the party, Baby Samuel announced that the Chens from Far End would bring all the food and drinks for his party, and that the Knabers would help the Chens to arrange the food and drinks and bring them to the party from Far End.

The day of the big party was cold and rainy, but the people of First End were cheerful because they needed the rain more than they needed a sunny Baby Samuel party! But people from Middle End and Far End were less cheerful because Baby Samuel was such a 'big' and important friend and they didn't want anything to spoil his party.

Soon Baby Samuel's house started filling up with guests. After all, Baby Samuel this time invited almost everybody in VillageAll. The Chens were already there, there were so many of them and they seemed to be in control of things.

The Popovs arrived in a cloud of spray with Mr Popov's roaring laughter startling everybody, and Mr Chen said to his wife, "It is good that Mr Popov is still laughing since he has nothing to laugh about." Then the Watanabes arrived, with Mrs Watanabe clutching her husband's arm tightly with one hand, and with the other hand clutching the food she brought with her. Mrs Watanabe had said to her husband that although the Chens could make good food, she was not sure if the Knabers could.

When everybody had arrived, Baby Samuel's giant house was quite full. Baby Samuel was going around smiling and murmuring greetings, and everybody was waiting for the party to start. Even though there was a lot of food and lots of drinks and many people, nobody felt there was a party because although everybody wanted to have a party with Baby Samuel, more than that, and with or without a party, everybody wanted to see the Knabers.

Well, almost everybody, because Mrs Smith, who had seen them before and didn't much like them, said Knabers do not make a party, and should not break one either.

Well, the big rooms of Baby Samuel's house were very crowded, and although everybody kept looking for them, nobody could see the Knabers, and Mrs Pompidou said to her husband, "Mr Smith's little friends have come to the party but the party has gone to them and now we have neither Knabers nor party." Mr Pompidou said that, well, the Knabers were so little and were very good at doing things while hiding.

While everybody was looking down for the Knabers, some of the women in the party were looking up and started noticing strange things. Mrs Schmidt said that she thought the ceiling of the house looked higher than it was at the time of Baby Samuel's second birthday party, and Mrs De Graff said that she thought the doors looked bigger than before, and Mrs Kim said that she thought the windows looked higher than before.

Other women started noticing also, and then the women told their husbands, and the husbands started looking and talked to their friends, and soon the party was very quiet as everybody was looking up.

Baby Samuel, looking down from high above the crowd, suddenly saw all those faces looking up towards him. He was so pleased, and with a huge grin started singing, "Happy birthday to me…" He waved his arms to get everybody to join him.

At last the party seemed to have started and the house became very noisy with everybody eating, drinking, and chatting to everybody else.

In the middle of the party, Baby Samuel sat in his giant chair, which looked just a little too big. He was fidgety and didn't seem to know what to do or where to look, and Mrs Pompidou said to her husband, "Baby Samuel looks tired and bored. He has also grown smaller. This Baby Samuel is very different from the Baby Samuel who celebrated his second birthday."

And Mr Pompidou said he could not agree more.

In the days after Baby Samuel's birthday party a mist enveloped VillageAll. And the mood of VillageAll people was quiet and hazy like the mist.

Everybody wanted to know what would happen when Baby Samuel got even smaller. What would happen to New End, and the noria wheel? Who would be big enough to deal with the Knabers?

Well, almost everybody, because the Chens and the Singhs already knew.

The Chens and Singhs and many of their friends knew that when the mist lifted they could take care of the Noria Wheel. They knew that nobody was big enough to deal with the Knabers.

They knew that Baby Samuel would still take care of New End and that perhaps VillageAll on *this* side of the river did not need New End, just like it once did not have to.

NOTES

1.   United Kingdom
2.   France
3.   Germany
4.   Italy
5.   Holland
6.   Sweden/Scandinavia
7.   Spain
8.   Greece
9.   Russia
10.   Natives of 'undiscovered' lands, especially American Indians
11.   Ottomans (Turkey)
12.   Arabia (Middle Eastern Arab countries)
13.   Persia (Iran)
14.   India
15.   African nations
16.   Slave trade in the 16th & 17th centuries
17.   China
18.   Korea
19.   Vietnam
20.   Thailand
21.   Indonesia
22.   Burma (Myanmar)

23.   Cambodia
24.   Japan
25.   Japan was virtually isolated from the rest of the
        world during the Tokugawa (Edo) era- from
        early 17th century till mid-19th century
26.   British-French Colonial Wars
27.   European religious discord
28.   The Industrial Revolution c. 1760
29.   Russo-Turkish Wars 1768-74
30.   Jamestown 1607
31.   The Boston Tea Party 1773
32.   American War of Independence
33.   The French Revolution
34.   Napoleonic Wars
35.   British Supremacy in India
36.   British-American War 1812-1814
37.   War of Independence in Latin America 1811-26
38.   Trail of Tears: 1838- More than 15,000
        Cherokee Indians were forced to march from
        Georgia to Indian Territory in present-day
        Oklahoma. Approximately 4,000 die from
        starvation and disease
39.   Mexican War between USA and Mexico 1845-
        46
40.   Crimean War 1853-56
41.   The Opening of Japan; Commodore Perry's
        Black Ships 1854
42.   Opium War Britain and China 1839-1942
43.   Taiping Rebellion 1850-64 : political and
        religious uprising that ravaged seventeen
        Chinese provinces and cost twenty million lives

44. Anglo-Chinese War 1856-60
45. Economic & Financial crisis 1857
46. Bankers: finance, the financial institutions
47. American Civil War 1861–1865
48. Japan's Meiji Restoration 1868
49. Japanese-Korean Treaty secures Korean independence from China 1876
50. Sino-French War 1884-1885
51. The Statue of Liberty: a gift to the United States from the people of France to memorialize the alliance of the two countries in the American Revolution and their abiding friendship. The French people contributed the $250,000 cost
52. Wounded Knee Massacre: last major battle of the Indian Wars at Wounded Knee in South Dakota
53. Sino-Japanese War 1894-95
54. Russo-Japanese War 1904-05
55. World War one 1914-1918
56. Russian Revolution 1917-1923 and Russian Civil War 1917-22
57. USSR: Union of Soviet Socialist Republics
58. The BBC
59. 'Black Tuesday'; onset of Wall Street Crash and the great depression 1929
60. The Holocaust
61. Balfour Declaration gives British support to a Jewish homeland in Palestine 1917
62. Japan Manchurian War 1931-1932
63. World War Two 1939-1945
64. Foundation of the State of Israel